Just Witch It

Erin Bedford

Also by Erin Bedford

The Underground Series
Chasing Rabbits
Chasing Cats
Chasing Princes
Chasing Shadows
Chasing Hearts
The Crimes of Alice

The Mary Wiles Chronicles
Marked by Hell
Bound by Hell
Deceived by Hell
Tempted by Hell

Starcrossed Dragons
Riding Lightning
Grinding Frost
Swallowing Fire
Pounding Earth

The Celestial War Chronicles
Song of Blood and Fire

The Crimson Fold
Until Midnight
Until Dawn
Until Sunset
Until Twilight

<u>**Curse of the Fairy Tales**</u>
Rapunzel Untamed
Rapunzel Unveiled

<u>**Her Angels**</u>
Heaven's Embrace
Heaven's A Beach
Heaven's Most Wanted

<u>**House of Durand**</u>
Indebted to the Vampires
Wanted by the Vampires
Protected by the Vampires

<u>**Academy of Witches**</u>
Witching On A Star
As You Witch
Witch You Were Here
Just Witch It
Summer Witchin'

Granting Her Wish
Vampire CEO

Just Witch It

Erin Bedford

Chapter 1

MY BACK SMACKED AGAINST the bookcase, jostling a few tomes out of their place. They fell to the floor with a loud thwack, making me pull my lips away from Ian's addicting mouth for a second to scowl.

"Quiet. Do you want to get caught?" My eyes darted around the library of Winchester Academy before locking with Ian's hooded hazel eyes.

"Do you really think I'm worried about getting caught?" Ian's lips curved up in a smirk as he slid his hand farther up my skirt to cup my heat between my legs. I groaned as his thumb circled me through the material. "Shh, now, Max, you don't want to get caught, do you?"

As if to add insult to injury, my guardian light, Aris, bobbed around our heads. I took that to mean he agreed with Ian, the little twat.

I tried to give Ian an exasperated look as he parroted my words back at me, but Ian had chosen that moment to push my panties aside and plunge his fingers into my needy cavern. I bit my lip as I tried to hold in a groan, my head falling back against the bookshelf, knocking a few more books down, but I didn't care this time.

Ian's molten, mesmerizing eyes watched me with desire, His hand moving beneath my skirt while the other was propped up by my head. I grabbed hold of his black t-shirt, twisting my fingers in the soft material as he flicked my clit one more time, causing me to come undone.

"Merlin, I could watch you come all day," Ian murmured against my lips as he kissed me.

I kissed him back with eagerness, pushing my heavy chest against him. "I could have you make me come all day..." I shoved him back with a grin and a wink. "But not in the library."

I left him staring as I sashayed down the many aisles of books, knowing full well that he was watching me walk away. He wouldn't wait long. In fact, three, two, one...

Ian threw an arm around my shoulder and pulled me close. "Then let's go find somewhere more private and I'll make you come on my face."

I flushed at his words as my eyes darted around the library to see if anyone had heard, but no one was even paying us any mind. They were too busy with either their studies or socializing to care what we were doing. Last year, it might have been a big deal, but the students of Winchester Academy had gotten over the tasty gossip that was my relationship with not just one of the wizards who attended here, but four.

Not to say there weren't still a few who didn't approve, my grandmother for one. Nina Mancaster cared about what people thought, so that meant I had to act the good witch and not cause a scandal. Fat chance when three out of the four wizards I was dating were high society wizards. Ian Broomstein was only one of the two Broomstein brothers, and I was dating both him and his brother Paul. In fact, my grandmother should be happy that I kept my escapades in the bedroom. Imagine the shock and horror she would feel if she knew I'd been with both brothers at the same time.

My eyes glazed over, and my body warmed even more from the memory of Paul thrusting into me from behind as I sucked on Ian's cock. His long, hard, pierced cock. A small shiver of delight went through me.

"Cold?" Ian glanced down at me, arching a brow.

I grinned and shook my head. "No, just remembering... things." My eyes dropped to his crotch where he still had a slight hard-on.

Ian must have guessed what I'd been thinking because the heat in his eyes grew, making my nipples hard. "Well, then let's go to my room and we can... reminisce together."

My thighs rubbed together as I eagerly nodded. Ian grabbed my hand and led me out of the library. I giggled and glanced around as our footsteps quickened. We were both eager to get to his room, it seemed.

We rushed down the hallway, pushing past students and teachers alike, in our hurry to his room. Trina, my roommate, stood by her girlfriend Libby in the quad, with her ebony hair in braids. When her dark eyes caught sight of me, she tried to get me to stop and talk to her, but I shook my head and grinned at her. Her eyes widened and then she mimed sucking a dick before bursting out laughing with Libby.

I shook my head at her antics and turned back to follow Ian. He led us down the sophomore hallway, where my room was this year, and into another corridor I'd never been in before. Each hallway was assigned to different years, and on top of that, some of them were reserved for more elite families. Fortunately, or not, it depended on the day really, I was part of one of those families. Ian was too, but as we came closer to his room, I realized I'd never been to his dorm room before.

My feet slowed as I took in the differences between my hallway and Ian's. While mine had at least a dozen doors on each side, his only had about half of that in the whole corridor. It made me wonder what was behind those doors that they would need so much more space.

"What's wrong?" Ian squeezed my hand, pulling my attention to him. He cocked his head to the side, which made his dark hair fall into his wicked eyes.

I smiled, and as I reached up to brush his hair out of his face, I admitted, "I just realized I've never been to your room before."

Ian angled his head to the side and hummed. "Oh, I guess you haven't." He gave me a wicked grin before wagging his brows. "Well, now I may not let you leave."

I laughed and smacked his chest. "Just show me which one of these is yours. I have to meet Callie for dinner tonight."

Ian pretended to pout. I wanted to bite that lip. "I see how it is. Get what you want from me and then go out with her."

"Oh, yeah." I rolled my eyes sarcastically. "I totally want in Callie's pants, but don't tell her that. She'll never let you live it down.

She's already jealous of all of you taking up all my time."

Ian pulled me close for a moment, and his hand went to my ass. "Well, I'm about to take up even more of your time, and..." His hands slid lower until it was beneath my skirt. He squeezed my ass cheek, his fingers teasing between my legs. "Other places, real soon."

While my body wanted very much for him to push me up against the hallway wall and show me what he meant right then, a trio of students came by, their eyes locked on us with interest. I ducked my head and shifted out of his grasp. Reluctantly, Ian released me before jerking his head with a grin to the passersby.

"What's up? Great weather we're having, huh?"

One of the females in the group giggled while another gave me a glare. Jealous much?

Once they were out of sight, Ian grabbed my hand once more. "Come on, before I give these innocent people a show and fuck you right here in the hallway."

Oh, Merlin. The things he said. I could explode right here with just his words alone. Sometimes, I was a little in awe of how I seemed to snag the attention of such a sexy and cool guy. I mean, back in high school I wasn't unpopular, but I'd never have gotten attention from someone like Ian. Paul or Dale would have been more up my alley—safe, nice guys who wouldn't give my dad a heart attack on first meeting.

Still, some of the wicked things I've done with those two would probably give my dad a stroke if he knew. I giggled at the thought.

"Laugh now, Mancaster." Ian grinned over his shoulder at me as we stopped at one of the doors in the hallway. "You won't be doing much of anything but screaming my name soon."

I giggled even more and smoothed my hand up the back of his shirt. "That's what you think."

As he shoved the door open, Ian lifted me up by the ass. I threw my head back and laughed, wrapping my legs around his waist. His mouth found its way onto my neck in the one place he knew made my knees weak. My laughter died off, and I clenched my legs around him now for a whole different reason.

Ian lowered me down to the couch... Couch? Where'd that come from? He wasted no time kneeling before me. I'd barely opened my eyes to look around before Ian had my panties off, discarded somewhere, and buried his face between my thighs. My eyes caught sight of a television before I squeezed them closed again as Ian lapped at my folds.

"Ian," I groaned out, and tangled my fingers into his dark hair. My hips jerked up off the midnight blue couch, trying to get closer to him. He pinned my hips down with his hands and sucked my clit into his mouth. I let out a squeal as I fought against him by pulling at his hair. Either to pull him closer or to push him away, it was just too much, too intense. I couldn't breathe. I couldn't think.

When I came apart this time, Ian didn't stop. Though he released my clit, Ian slid his tongue along my folds and teased my entrance. His hands moved from my hips, one pushing my shirt up so he could cup my breast, while the other replaced his mouth at my center. My eyes flipped open to see his face before mine, so I pulled him toward me by the front of his shirt. As Ian drew closer, he lunged forward the rest of the way to capture my mouth, his tongue wasting no time plunging into my mouth as his fingers were exploring inside me down below.

"Ah, Ian," I gasped into his mouth, my hands jerking at his shirt as I tried to get it off him. "Naked. Now."

I could feel him smiling against my mouth before he mumbled, "Magic, Maxine. Magic."

Taking a deep breath, I focused my magic on what I wanted. I'd never used it to get naked. Especially, not someone else at the same time. I was partly worried I'd end up turning us inside out. That would put a real damper on the night.

Pushing away my nerves, I envisioned myself naked first. My clothes disappeared from my form and Ian hummed appreciatively, fingers curling around my hips as his eyes gobbled up my bare flesh. If I wasn't already hot and ready for him, I sure as hell was now.

"Now, your turn." I licked my lips and grabbed at his shirt, pushing magic into my fingers and out into Ian's clothes. Like breathing, in one exhale, his clothes disintegrated.

"Finally," Ian breathed, rubbing his chest against mine. My nipples pebbled and I wiggled against him.

I could finally touch his warm skin. I gripped his muscular back, my nails scratching along his shoulder blades as I widened my legs and tried to pull him closer. Ian wouldn't budge. Instead, he removed his hand from between my thighs, I whimpered at the emptiness, and lifted me from the couch once more.

"Where are we going?" I asked between kisses.

"My bed," he growled.

Those words were enough to make me even more ready for him, only adding to the fact that every step he took made my heat rub against the hard planes of his abs as his hardened length bumped against my butt. I heard him kick a door open, and this time I pushed back the desire to have him inside me to look around the room.

Ian's room reminded me of him in the most elemental way. Dark curtains covered the windows to block out the sun, thin rays still managing to stream in between them. Silk sheets covered his bed in a forest green. The matching nightstand and dresser were made of dark mahogany wood, and my fingers itched to go through it. Ian was an enigma, but after a year with him, I didn't know as much about him as I wanted. The fact that this was the first time I'd ever been to his room was a telling sign of how private of a person Ian was. He didn't even have much laying out on his desk besides books and school supplies. It made him even more dark and mysterious.

"See something that interests you?" he whispered.

I met Ian's gaze as my lips ticked up at the sides. "You have quite a lot of pillows for a Dark Arts major." I jerked my head back to the bed where more than six pillows were piled on top of the comforter.

Ian chuckled and lowered me to the bed so my head fell back on several of those fluffy pillows. "What makes you think I didn't get them for you?"

My heart warmed, even as I rolled my eyes. "Sure, you did. You just don't want anyone to know what a big softy you are underneath all that bad boy exterior."

Ian grabbed my hand and put it on his cock, squeezing my hand under his firmly. "Does this feel like I'm soft to you?"

I licked my lips and shook my head as I stared at the reddened top of his cock. Our hands moved up and down his shaft together, and on each trip, our fingers brushed over the silver barbell pierced through the skin there.

"Did that hurt?" I blurted out, pulling my hand from his to trace the metal line until it disappeared beneath the surface.

Ian hissed through his teeth but let me touch him at my leisure. "At the time, yes, but it's worth it."

"Is it?" I glanced up from his piercing to his face as I spoke.

His lips curled up into a lopsided smirk. "Let me show you."

Ian pushed my hand away, gripping his length as he adjusted his approach to just the right angle. He teased my entrance with the tip, dipping in slightly before pulling away. He did it enough times that I was panting and ready to take over for him, but before I could, without warning, he plunged his full length inside of me.

My back arched off the bed, and I let out a startled sound. My fingers curled around his biceps as I tried to catch my breath. Then Ian

17

began to move, and I was gone. That little metal bar rubbed inside of me, touching all the places I'd never been able to get to myself, and before I knew it, my toes were curling under and I was screaming Ian's name.

Ian gave me a smug grin after we finished, and he slipped out of me. "See? Told you."

I panted and patted his shoulder weakly. "Yes, yes. You're fabulous."

We lay there in his bed for a few more moments with only the sound of our breathing filling the room. It was like that with Ian. I didn't have to talk to fill the void of silence. We could just be with each other without having to go somewhere fancy or pretend to be having fun at some public event. He never made me feel like I had to be something I wasn't, not like the rest of my wizarding family.

Determined not to let my family drama ruin this moment, I let my eyes wander his room once more. There was something I missed before, a large black case with stickers covering it. I sat up and pointed to the case.

"What's that?"

Ian blinked his eyes open and lazily turned over to see what I was pointing at. "Oh, that? That's my gun for the games."

"Games?"

"You know, the MagiX Games. I'm competing this year." He waved a hand nonchalantly in the air, but I was up and off the bed.

I sauntered over to the case and traced my fingers over some of the stickers. Some were just team logos while others said things like, 'Hazard: Badass Incoming,' and 'Potions or Die.' I fingered the clasps and glanced over my shoulder at Ian.

"Can I see it?"

Ian sat up on his elbows and arched a brow. "You haven't seen enough of me already?"

"Not your dick." I rolled my eyes at him. "The gun, idiot."

"Isn't it one and the same?" Ian gave me a lopsided grin as he climbed off the bed and knelt next to me, completely at ease with his nakedness, thank Merlin.

When Ian popped the case open, I jerked my eyes away from his delicious form to the contents. Inside sat a gun like the one Trina had shoved in her bag when we first arrived this year, except this one was way nicer. Like most of Ian's things, it was black with blue accents, and reminded me of a paintball gun, with a hopper for the balls mounted on the back of it.

"So, these games," I started, looking from his gun to him, "is it just paintball?"

"Potion Ball," Ian corrected me before he closed the case with a snap and stood. "And no. There are several games. Broom racing—"

I laughed, interrupting him. "Broom racing? Really?" I stood with him and cocked my head to the side.

Ian tipped my chin up and kissed the end of my nose. "Of course, we are nothing if not traditional." I grinned at him as he continued, "Then there's the spellcasting event and then it ends with a massive game of Potion Ball."

I stood, my eyes still on the case. "And anyone can enter to play?"

"Are you thinking of entering, Max?" Ian crossed his arms over his chest and lifted a brow.

Shrugging a shoulder, I glanced over at him. "What if I am?"

A broad grin spread across Ian's lips, before he stated, "Then before we get you your very own gun, I better teach you how to use it."

"I already know how to use it," I said with a smirk.

Ian frowned for a moment, but when I arched an eyebrow at his quickly hardening cock, he broke into a laugh. "Haha, that you do. That you do."

Chapter 2

SADLY, ALL GOOD THINGS must come to an end. Eventually, we were spent, and as we collected ourselves, Ian put his shirt back on and hid his mouth-watering abs from view. I finished getting dressed myself, and we made our way out of his room and into the living room area he'd briefly stopped us in before.

Now that my head wasn't clouded with sex, I could check out the room around me. Out here it was a bit brighter, like whoever decorated it didn't want you to see the darkness hidden in his bedroom. The walls were cream with a tan accent, the furniture white to offset the dark couch. There was another desk in here, as well as a large flat screen television. Ian's laptop was sitting on the desk, the screensaver a slideshow of images—potions, motorcycles, and one of us together.

"When did you take that?" I pointed at the computer as I moved closer to it. I had my blonde hair down and my head was thrown back as I laughed. Ian was smiling with his arms around me, the corner of his eyes crinkled. We looked so happy.

Ian rubbed the back of his neck and seemed embarrassed. "Uh, I didn't. Paul did."

"Paul?" I glanced back at him. "Didn't figure him for one to snap pictures without making a big production of it."

Slipping his arm around my waist, Ian tugged me to his side before placing a kiss on the side of my neck. "We all have sides of us we don't show to others. You seem to just bring them out in us."

I leaned into his embrace, wrapping one arm around his neck, and I peered up at him. I liked this. Being in his arms. Not having to worry about if anyone was watching or if someone was going to snap a picture of us for *Witch Weekly*. I loved dating all four of my guys, but sometimes it was just tiring. You'd think that they'd find something else to report on, but apparently the only heir to the Mancaster legacy dating four wizards was still hot news. I wished someone else would grab the spotlight for once.

"So, about that gun?" I asked, a bit more excited about a weapon, even one for a sport, than I thought I would be. "When can I get one?"

"All in good time." Ian chuckled and flicked my nose. "I messaged Aidan to meet us down in the quad."

"Aidan?" I pulled away from him, lacing my fingers with his as we headed to the door. "He's in the games too?"

Ian raised his brows. "You really don't know Aidan that well, do you?"

I frowned. Unfortunately, he was right. Out of the four of them, Aidan was the hardest one to get to know. While Ian was a mystery I loved unraveling every single day, Aidan was an enigma. His stoic personality made it like pulling teeth to get more than a two-word answer out of him, and he rarely offered up information about himself. He certainly had never said anything about something like this. It made me want to dig my heels in and find out everything I could.

"So, he plays Potion Ball too?"

Ian opened the bedroom door for me and ushered us outside. The hallways were a bit more crowded now that it was closer to dinnertime. Classes started again tomorrow, so everyone was getting as much socializing in as possible before they had to put their nose into their books.

"Aidan doesn't just play Potion Ball." Ian snort-laughed. "He dominates it."

My face scrunched up in confusion. "Huh?"

"You know, he's one of those guys who takes sports really seriously," Ian continued, as we passed by my hallway. We were almost to the quad now.

"Oh." I chewed on my lower lip. "That's surprising. I didn't figure him for the type, but I guess he has all those muscles for a reason."

The wizard in question came into view and surprisingly, he was surrounded by female students... or I guess I shouldn't be surprised. Aidan Templar was hot. He had that 'suffer in silence' kind of thing about him that added to the appeal of those startling blue eyes and beefy muscles. Any girl would want him at her side.

Aidan was the only one of the guys I hadn't slept with yet, now that Ian and I had finally gone all the way. We'd done stuff, sure, but usually one of the other guys was there, most often Ian. Those two seemed to be a package deal. You'd think it would be Ian and Paul, but besides the one time we got together at my grandmother's house, they didn't like to touch me at the same time. Sibling issues.

Today though, Aidan looked even more tempting than usual. He lacked his usual video game logo t-shirt, and instead wore a white ribbed tank top, and jeans that hugged his thighs and biteable ass. He had his arms crossed over his chest and wasn't even pretending to care what the female fluttering her eyelashes at him was chattering about.

When Aidan noticed me, those bright blue eyes locked onto me, and I swear I melted into a puddle right there. He pushed through the gaggle of student admirers, not the least bit bothered by their cries of annoyance on his way over to me. Aidan stopped before me, then one of his large hands cupped the side of my face.

I leaned into it, grasping his hand with both of mine as I kept it there and murmured, "Those girls are contemplating my death."

"What girls?" he said so matter-of-factly that, if I hadn't already been into him, I'd have fallen for him right then.

"Come on, Romeo." Ian smacked Aidan on the back. "Max wants to learn how to shoot for the games." His gaze swung to me for a second. "What time do you have to meet Callie for dinner?"

I ripped my eyes away from Aidan to look at my phone time. "Uh, crap. Now." I winced and gave them an apologetic smile. "Sorry, I really want to learn how, but I promised her I'd go to dinner with her." Ian opened his mouth, but I cut him off. "Girls only, no boyfriends." I gave a helpless shrug. "I'll make it up to you?"

Aidan let out a growl and pulled me flush against his front. My chin came to his chest, and he lifted me with both hands on my ass as he crushed his mouth to mine. I wrapped my arms around his neck, sliding my fingers into the short ends of his hair. He'd been growing it longer, and I wondered if it was for me. I mean, I had a thing for long hair. I didn't know why, I just wanted to stick my hands in it and pull.

Before we could get too carried away, Ian laughed and teased, "Alright, just bone already so we can get rid of this tension." I withdrew from Aidan to see Ian wave a hand in front of his face. "It's so thick, it's giving my dick a complex."

I grinned at Aidan and pecked him on the lips one final time before he lowered me back to the ground. Turning to Ian, I grabbed him by the shirt and gave him a quick, passionate kiss before releasing him with a wink.

"That should tide your dick over."

Ian not so subtly adjusted himself, not caring that we're in the middle of the quad and had already attracted attention. "Fucking doubt it." With a dramatic sigh, he waved me away. "Go, go, before I find a broom closet to drag you into."

I giggled at that and waved before spinning on my heels. Walking with my head high, mainly because I knew I was getting dirty looks, I kept my eyes forward and a smug smile on my lips. Eat your heart out, Winchester Academy.

Callie, thankfully, was already waiting in the U-shape driveway in the front of campus in her cherry red convertible. Her dark hair was braided and hanging over one shoulder, while her big brown eyes were covered by her large framed sunglasses. She wore an off-the-shoulder purple sweater and a pair of white capris, with three-inch heels. How she could even drive, let alone walk in those things all day, was beyond my comprehension.

"What's with the sunglasses?" I gestured to them as I slid into the passenger seat. "It's almost dark out."

Callie grinned and shrugged a shoulder as she pulled out of the academy's U-shaped drive. "Us plain humans have to make our own mystery where we can. How else am I going to bag myself a wizard?"

I laughed and shook my head. "By being your own spectacular self."

"They get to do magic." Callie snorted. "Being with me is already going to be boring as it is. The most I can do is get out of a speeding ticket." With that, she drove us down the street toward our favorite burger place, McKee's.

I didn't know Callie felt that way. I knew that ever since I decided not to go to Brown with her, she'd felt a bit left out, something compounded when she learned that I was a witch. But she rebounded as she always did, and became really excited about getting to be best friends with a witch and joked about wanting to nab herself a wizard… but I didn't realize how insecure she'd been feeling about the whole thing.

"Oh, Callie." I wrapped my arm around her shoulders and tried to hug her as much as I could while she was driving. "Those guys don't want another boring old witch."

Callie scoffed, and if she hadn't been wearing sunglasses, I was sure she'd have been rolling her eyes at me.

"I mean it, they see magic every single day, but having to do things without magic?" I grinned at her. "Have you seen one of them try to work a blender the old-fashioned way? Seriously, it's hilarious."

Callie lowered her sunglasses to give me an unamused look. "Really, now? A blender? They can stop time. What the hell do they care about blenders?"

"But Callie," I tried again, as she parked us in the lot of McKee's, "those witch girls use a ton of short cuts... for everything." I wagged my brows to try to get my point across.

It took her a second to catch on, but then her mouth slowly dropped open. "You mean, they don't know how to give a decent blow job? What do they do, just cast a spell on the guy's dick?"

I lifted a shoulder. "I don't know for sure, but Ian told me he almost got his junk spelled off once because the girl was too worried about germs to blow him."

Callie had a contemplative look on her face, and for a second, I felt bad. I was lying through my teeth, but I figured something like that wasn't too far off. Besides, this was my best friend. I couldn't let her sink into despair because of her not-so-magical life.

I grabbed her bag and tossed it to her before getting out of the car. "Besides, what about Professor Morison? I thought you were talking to him?"

"Rupert is hot and all, you know me and British accents," Callie climbed out of the car and slung her large purse over her shoulder with a grimace, "but I don't know. He's quite a bit older than me. We don't have a lot in common."

I hummed and pulled the door to McKee's open. The busy sounds of customers and the kitchen filled my ears right before the scent of freshly made burgers and fries hit my nose. Merlin, I loved food.

"Well, have you even gone on a date yet?"

I stopped at the greeter's sign and waited to be seated. McKee's had that fifties diner vibe going for it, with vinyl seats in red and white, and even a classic jukebox salvaged from an auction pushed up against the back wall. Callie and I loved to come here, but lately I'd been... busy. It was hard to juggle my human life with my magical one, especially when you added four boyfriends to the mix. Once we got to my best friend and her needs, I was sure I was one incident away from having a meltdown.

"Of course, we've gone on a date," Callie replied, flipping her hair over her shoulder. "If you call making out in his car after going to the drive-in a date."

"Hey, ladies." Pamela, a chipper single mom who worked the evening shift, bounced over, her hair a glossy shade of black and purple. "Having a girls' night?"

"You know it, Pam." Callie beamed at her as she looped her arm through mine. "No boys tonight. Just me and my main squeeze." She gripped my arm tighter and tighter until I winced.

"Hey, your main squeeze is still breakable, you know." I withdrew my arm from her and rubbed the sore spot. To Pamela, I asked, "Can we get a booth, please? In the back?"

Pamela arched a drawn-on brow but didn't question it. Most people who asked for a back booth were couples who wanted to be alone. Callie and I usually sat at the bar top where we could order pie, and sit there and pretend we were in the actual fifties. However, Callie and I had things to talk about... magical things, and I couldn't take the chance of one of the workers or customers eavesdropping on us.

"Okay, right this way." Pamela turned on her white tennis shoes, her pastel pink Capris, and white and pink polka dot blouse really playing into the theme of the place.

Callie and I moved into our booth, the vinyl squeaking as we slid against it. We grabbed our menus from the condiment rack on the table and pretended to look them over. We always got the same thing every time we came, but far be it for us to look predictable.

After a moment, we both turned to Pamela and said, "Burger, fries, and a—"

"Chocolate milkshake, extra whip," Pamela finished for us with a grin and a wink. "Don't say that I don't know my girls."

"Never," Callie gasped, placing her hand on her chest with mock horror.

"Wouldn't dream of it," I added with a nod, then asked, "How's little Hailey doing?"

"Great!" Pamela beamed. "She'll be started second grade this year. Of course, after spending the summer with her dad, she can't stop going on about the puppy his new girlfriend has." We winced in sympathy. "Think that means I'm going to have to give in and get her one soon."

"Make her take care of a goldfish first," Callie told her with a serious tone. "That way she knows it's a big responsibility, not just something cool Daddy has that you don't."

"Good idea, Cal." Pamela bumped her with her elbow and winked. "I knew I liked you for a reason."

Callie gave a small smile. "Ten years of playing the divorcée's kid will teach you a few things. Let me know when she starts to play the 'but daddy lets me do it' card. I always used that one."

We laughed as Pamela excused herself to put in our order. Once she was gone, I grabbed Callie's hands.

"Cal, I have some news."

Callie's eyes narrowed in suspicion. "You better not be pregnant. I so don't want to be on the magical version of Jerry Springer's 'I'm not the daddy.'"

I rolled my eyes and smacked her hands. "No, I'm not pregnant, and besides, it'd only be three guys to contend for anyway."

"No, it wouldn't. Dale and Paul. Ian doesn't count as having a threesome since you only sucked him off." I stared at her hard, wondering how I could be friends with someone so dense. Then Callie's eyes widened, her mouth dropped, and she smacked the table so loud the neighboring tables looked our way. "You did it with someone else? Who? Who? Please tell me it was Ian. No, Aidan." Her eyes got all starry. "I always wanted to know what it would be like with someone built like him. He could lift you up and move you around like a rag doll, and you wouldn't even have to break a sweat."

I giggled at her theatrics. "Sorry, not yet."

"So, it was Ian?"

I nodded, holding back a grin.

Callie let out a high-pitched squeal and jumped up in her seat to call out to Pamela. "We need some pie over here, stat!" As she dropped back into her seat, she grabbed my hands and leaned in conspiratorially. "Tell me everything."

Chapter 3

"MAXINE, DARLING," MY GRANDMOTHER crooned in my ear, as I held my phone up against my face and shoulder.

I pulled it away for a second, putting it on speakerphone, before sitting it on my desk as I jerked on my pale yellow, V-neck shirt and tucked a hand in my jeans pocket, prepared for what was probably another lecture about my recent coming out. "Your coming out was a smashing success, besides the tiny hiccup with that awful Magenski girl. Still, that was easily forgotten aside from when your cousin, Addy, bumped into one of the Sage men and caused that whole ruckus at the buffet table." She let out a little laugh. "I've never seen so many guests having to spell cake and lobster pate off themselves in my life!"

My second year at Winchester Academy had already started, and after the summer, no one wanted to get back to normal more than me. Well, as normal as one could get when you were a human turned witch just now getting her feet wet in the wizardry world.

My lips curled up at the edges where I stood by my dorm room window. "Yeah, I heard about that. Sorry I missed it."

My grandmother made a sound in her throat, a cross between a snort and a laugh—well, if Nina Mancaster could act so low to make such a sound.

"Yes, don't think I didn't notice you skipping out on your own party to do Merlin knows what with those boys of yours."

"And you had nothing to do with their surprise either?" I teased and giggled.

My coming out party hadn't just been for the benefit of my grandmother and the wizarding society, but also for my birthday. What had been a clusterfuck of mean girl sabotage had turned into a wonderful night to remember. The guys had whisked me away to a secret party in the middle of the pond behind my grandparents' mansion. We had cake, fireworks, and enough laughter to hold me over for the rest of the year.

My grandmother made a humming, pleased sound that pulled my attention out of my thoughts. "Yes, well. While I admit the thought of you dating four boys was appalling at first, they do care for you and know how to keep you happy." She made a small, amused hum. "Who knows? Maybe I'll see about gaining a few extra beaus myself."

"Grandmother!" I gaped at the phone, my cheeks hurting from how wide my smile had gotten. "What about Grandfather?"

She made a little clicking noise with her mouth, and I could just imagine the haughty expression on her face. "Your grandfather is the love of my life, but he might appreciate some help with the load at times. We aren't getting any younger, you know. It's as good of a time as any to take chances."

She paused for a moment and then, as if talking to herself, she murmured, "Perhaps we'll take up swinging."

"I'm not hearing this," I groaned and rubbed a hand down my face. "I choose to be blissfully ignorant of all of this."

"Oh, Maxine," she scoffed. "I'm only joking. I'd never..."

Ha. That's what she said, but the way she was going on about it made me wonder if she did want another set of hands or two. Either way, it wasn't something I wanted to think about. I had my own guys to worry about.

My heart warmed at that thought. My guys. Well, they certainly were. Who would have known that when I got the letter inviting me to Winchester Academy that it would come with such delicious perks? Certainly not me.

"In any case, we should talk about your next party," my grandmother continued, as if she hadn't just been talking about swinging with other couples. "Christmas will be coming in a few short months, and if we want to get a head start on things—"

I groaned and flopped down on the edge of my bed. "No. No more parties. Not for me. If you want to have one, go for it."

"But Maxine, it's just not the same—" Her words were cut off by a knock on my dorm room door.

I stood from the bed and headed to the door. "Grandmother, as much as I am enjoying this conversation, I have class. Can I call you later?"

I opened the door just as we said our goodbyes. With a grin, I leaned on the edge of the door to peer up at a pair of green eyes, Dale's eyes. I let my gaze drift down over Dale Varnes. His messenger bag hung across the front of his button-down shirt, the front pocket of which was filled with pens and God knows what else. Dale was a nerd but a hot one. Beneath his crisp white shirt and thick black glasses was a gloriously muscled beast, one that not only knew how to use his mouth to snap back at anyone who would dare challenge him to a battle of wits, but could also to send me into knee buckling, toe-curling bliss.

Right now, that mouth was tempting me something fierce. I stepped toward him and pressed my mouth to his. Our mouths melded together, and his tongue flicked out to slide against the seam of my lips. I eagerly granted him entry and pushed my front against him.

He'd cut his auburn hair recently, so it no longer fell completely in his face, but it was still long enough that I could tangle my fingers in it when we kissed. So that's what I did, tugging on a few strands until he let out a pleading moan to release him.

With a few deep breaths, I did so, stepping back from him to smile softly. "Hey, I was just heading out."

Dale pushed his glasses up his nose and gave me a lopsided grin, his mouth puffy from our kiss. "I know. We have the next class together."

My brows furrowed. "Uh, what?"

Dale and I were in different years. In fact, all my guys, except for Paul, were ahead of me in school. While Dale was only one year ahead, Ian and Aidan were scheduled to graduate and head out into the wide world at the end of this year, something I'd been trying not to think about too much.

Taking my question in stride, Dale took me by the arm and closed the door behind us as we stepped into the hallway. Pulling a piece of paper from his pocket, he unfolded it and handed it to me.

Right there on Monday, at three o'clock, he had the exact same class as me.

Pottery.

Why would a magical school even offer Pottery as an elective? I would think that when they had so many other fascinating things to teach us, they wouldn't even be offering bird courses—one you could fly right through—but seeing as I had finally caught up to the basics of being a witch, I actually had time to take classes outside of the core curriculum. So, pottery and broom flying were on my list of courses this year.

I know, right? Broom flying. I'd jumped into another world where I thought things like wand waving and broom flying were nonsense, but apparently, they're not. No, they were just old-fashioned, so of course when I saw it on the list of classes, I had to pick it.

Pottery, on the other hand, was more of me giving myself an easy A than anything else, but now that I knew Dale was in it with me, I was happy I picked it.

I clutched his arm and grinned happily as we walked down the hallway toward our classroom. A few people still gave us looks every once in a while, especially when I was with all four of them, but I was determined not to let it bother me.

"So, did we have a mind reading moment, or did you sneak a peek at my schedule?" I cocked a brow at him, giving Dale a sly grin.

Dale scratched his cheek with a finger as he glanced down at the floor. "I might have used my administrative privileges to find out what class I could take where I'd get to spend more time with you."

I grinned at his bashfulness and then scoffed, "And pottery was the only thing you could find? I have four other classes you could have stalked me in."

Dale rolled his eyes and wrapped his arm around my waist, so he could whisper in my ear. "But none of those require you to take a bath afterward."

My body heated and shuddered with desire. I pressed my thighs together and licked my lips at the prospect of showering with Dale. The last time we'd showered together had been more than a little fun and a whole lot of naughty.

"And besides," he kissed the side of my head, "I can't very well take magical herbalism and Advanced Potions two years in a row."

"And Arithmetic?" I sneaked a peek at him.

Dale lifted his eyes to the ceiling. "Numbers and I have a love-hate relationship that I am perfectly fine with."

I stopped him with a pull of his shirt, a smirk tugging at my lips. "And here I thought you were the nerdy one."

"Geek. Not nerd." Dale snorted and shook his head before lowering his face down to mine. "I don't play those little board games or whatnot... and not every geek is perfect at every subject. I'm better with dates and prose."

"What about broom flying?"

He shrugged sheepishly. "Scared of heights."

"That's okay." I pushed up on the toes of my tennis shoes and pecked him on the lips. "I have learned my way around a broom recently. I think I can drive for the both of us." I giggled and kissed him again.

"Is that right?" Dale chuckled, his pitch going low and husky the way I liked it. "Maybe after class you can give me a lesson?"

I snuck a glance around at the hallway mostly deserted by students already in their classes, and snuck my hand down to cup the hard-on beneath his slacks. He groaned and kissed me more feverishly as my hand gripped his length.

"Excuse me," a woman's voice cut in. "Are you coming in or not?"

Dale and I jerked apart, the hand that had been on his cock shoved behind my back. A woman with long, wavy hair and big glasses looked down at us without amusement. Her long nose was pointed in the air, and if she hadn't been wearing something straight out of the Sixties, she'd have given my grandmother a run for her money with her haughty gaze.

"Sorry, yes. We have this class." Dale cleared his throat, his face all business now, but the fine blush that covered his cheeks made me squeal on the inside.

I kept my mouth promptly shut and ducked my head, doing my best not to grin at being caught not only making out in the hallway, but well on our way to heavy petting. Could you say mortifying? I was so glad my grandmother wasn't here to see it. She'd be changing her tune about my wizards like that.

"Fine, then I suggest you take your seats." The hippy professor moved away from the door to allow Dale and I to duck in. We found two spots in the back of the room that were miraculously empty and next to each other. The other fifteen students in the class gave us curious looks before facing the front.

Our hippy instructor stood before the class, and then with a wave of her hand, the marker at the whiteboard wrote out a name. "Mrs. Kitty Pottington."

Before any of us could laugh over the irony of her name and the class she taught, Mrs. Pottington slapped a ruler on her desktop. "Now that I have your attention... there will be no laughing or giggling of any kind. You may call me Kitty or Mrs. Pottington, nothing else." She surveyed the room, holding out her ruler as if it were a dowsing rod that could search out any perpetrators.

I met Dale's eyes with a sidelong glance and suppressed a grin, but before even a split-second had passed, Kitty slapped the ruler again.

"Eyes up front. Those of you who think that this will be a bird course or an easy A, you have come to the wrong place." She paused, and took a deep breath as if she needed to calm herself. When she spoke again, her voice took on a lilting dreamy quality to it. "Pottery is like making love. You must be gentle with your clay, mold it, shape it into something that will love you and others in return." Her loving expression hardened, and she slapped the ruler again. "There will be no hanky-panky."

A male with almost white hair raised a shaky hand. "Uh. Where's the pottery stuff?"

He had a point. The classroom had none of those wheel things or a stove to cook them in, not even a shelf for materials. There were only chairs, Mrs. Pottington's desk, and that was it.

Kitty didn't seem upset by the student's question. She grinned almost forcefully and approached him. "You want to touch the clay?"

The blond's eyes skittered around the room, and then he nodded hesitantly.

"Well, too bad!" She slapped the ruler against her thigh, and the sound of it made me wince. "You cannot touch the clay until you learn how to love the clay. Learn how to mold it and yourself so that your magic does not hurt it." She had a heartbreaking smile on her face as her hand opened in front of her as if someone were giving her a gift.

We stared at her quizzically. What the fuck was wrong with her? If I didn't know any better, I'd say Kitty was huffing a bit too much of that marijuana they loved so much.

"Now!" Kitty straightened up as her eyes moved like sharp lasers across the classroom. "We will begin with the basics—the creation of the first clay pot."

The room suppressed a groan... or at least, I know I did. So much for taking an easy class.

Chapter 4

TUESDAY WAS THE DAY of my broom flying lessons. The class was held out on the football field, which was weird because I didn't even know we had a team, let alone a field. The field was a bit different than the one back at the high school. It was bigger, for one. For another, there were several sets of extra lines and I had no idea what they were for. Asking wasn't even an option, because the teacher for this class had a broomstick shoved so far up his ass that he'd need a proctologist to remove it.

"Now, before we begin, everyone has to sign this release form," Coach Heathers announced in a Scottish accent, making him sound even angrier than he probably was. He handed out the forms as he walked down the line of students. A blue baseball cap was perched on his head, featuring the school's crest prominently on it—an owl with a scroll clasped in its claw—while doing nothing to hide the curly red hair underneath. He was pale, speckled with freckles, and wore a red t-shirt with the school logo on the left pocket that was shoved into his shorts. Knee-length socks covered his thick legs that he'd somehow been able to fit into his tennis shoes.

I'd seen him around campus more than a few times, usually talking to other teachers and athletes. I'd even saw him talking to Aidan once, but I didn't know which sport Aidan played until I'd talked to Ian about it. I realized I didn't know a lot about my large, stoic boyfriend. He was hot, sure. A good listener. And while he was a man of few words, Aidan was sweet. But what he did in his spare time? No idea.

I'd always thought video games were the only thing he was really into. I mean, he wore a gamer tee almost every single day, but then again, he definitely didn't have the typical gamer body, not with all those lovely rippling muscles that made those gamer tees look one flex away from ripping open.

Coach Heathers went on about safety and liability, while we quickly signed the waivers he had handed out. "Now, no one is allowed to fly above three feet until I have signed you off. Understood?" His fuzzy brows furrowed over his fierce eyes as he stared us down like we would fuck up and he knew it. "If I see you above three feet before I give you the go ahead, you are out. I don't care who your mommy or daddy is, you got it?" His eyes shot to a few select students. Unfortunately, one of those was me.

I didn't want to let my grandparents' name effect how others treat me, but for some reason the more I protested, the more people treated me differently. I'd given up by this point.

Taking the form and pen that'd been handed out, I bent over and pressed it to my thigh, scrawling my name on the bottom of the form. I started to hand my waiver back, but the sound of a rolling cart drew my attention away from the scowling coach. Aidan—surprise, surprise—pushed a large metal cart on wheels filled with wooden brooms. My lips curled up as I caught sight of him and gave him a little wave.

Aidan, wearing gym shorts and a white tank top, inclined his head at me. His eyes smiled at me even if his lips barely moved. I noticed a few other women in the class checking him out, and my first instinct was to mark my territory. Before I could even think of how to do that, Coach Heathers snapped at us.

"Grab a broom and get on the twenty-yard line." Coach Heathers gestured wildly downfield before turning his back on us to flip through the signed forms.

Several females hurried over to the basket Aidan stood beside and fluttered their eyelashes at him. A brunette girl, with a nice figure and lashes that I would kill for, placed her hand on Aidan's bulging bicep. "Could you tell me where the twenty-yard line is?"

My eyes narrowed and my lips pressed into a thin line. I pushed my way through the crowd, prepared to show that girl exactly who Aidan belonged to, but I wasn't needed. Aidan shifted out of her grasp and pointed a finger across the field to the line nearby. He didn't even bother to say anything to her before he turned back to the crowd.

Happiness warmed my heart, and I waited with bated breath for my turn. When Aidan handed me a broom, our fingers brushed against one another and I smiled.

"Hey, I didn't know you were a teacher's aide too."

Aidan placed his hand on top of mine and gave me a little jerk to pull me close. My chest bumped against his stomach, and his musky, masculine scent filled my nostrils. "You never asked."

I beamed up at him, a bit breathless from our closeness. "I'll have to remedy that."

After brushing a strand of hair that had escaped from my ponytail back, Aidan ducked his head to brush his lips against mine. I sighed into the kiss. The brunette from before and a few others made disgusted sounds, and muttered something I didn't care to try to decipher, before dispersing around us.

"Templar, make out on your own time," Coach Heathers shouted. "I need your eyes on the air, not behind your eyelids."

As we parted, Aidan brushed his thumb across my cheek, and I leaned into his touch, pulling the edge of my lip between my teeth. When I finally moved to join my class at the twenty-yard line, Aidan smacked my ass. I jumped in place and shot him a look over my shoulder, but he had already turned to the next person in line. Shaking my head and laughing to myself, I took my place on the line.

The girl next to me fake coughed, "Slut."

I rolled my eyes and didn't bother to acknowledge the slight. Mature of me, right? Well, I wouldn't have been that way in high school, but when you're dating four guys, you kind of had to let things go. I'd already learned that the hard way with Sabrina. Who, for some weird reason, had now attached herself to me. Maybe it was because of Monica? I didn't know. Regardless, she was being nice, and that usually meant trouble. I just hoped it wasn't meant for me.

Coach Heathers walked down the line of students, his eyes scanning us as we held our broomsticks close. One guy was pretending like his broom was now his overly large dick, and Coach Heathers gave a small fake chuckle before grabbing the end of it and jerking it out of the guy's hands.

"This is not a toy," he growled. "It is not a substitute for your sad excuse of a dick, and it is not a sword nor any other kind of innuendo you sex-driven balls of hormones can think of. It is a mode of transportation," he barked at us in his Scottish accent, which might have been hot in his day, but now only made him sound like a hothead. "Now, you take your broom like so..." He held the guy's broom in front of his body with the handle parallel to the ground.

I held my broom out like Coach Heathers showed us. The others followed suit, none of them laughing now.

"Then, push the broom away from your palm and use your magic to make it hover." Coach Heathers did precisely that, making the broom float just below his hand.

The rest of us tried to follow him, but every single broom landed on the ground with a loud thwack. Groans and muttered curses filled the field as we tried again and again to get the broom to float.

"Come on, you pansies. It's a piece of wood, not a damn building. It can't be that hard." There were a few chuckles from the guys, but a single glare from Coach Heathers shut them up real quick.

I took a deep breath and blocked them all out. I grabbed at the ball of light inside of me, the source of my magic, and pushed it toward my hand, visualizing it going into the broom. On my next exhale, I uncurled my fingers from the broom and waited for the sound of the broom crashing to the ground.

Except this time, it didn't. There were a few gasps around me and I opened my eyes.

With a grin and a small squeal, I realized I'd done it. The broom hovered beneath my hand like it was being held up by strings. My head turned to the side to see how the others were doing and saw a few of them had gotten it as well. My heart swelled with delight, and I searched out Aidan, who hadn't left after handing out the brooms. His arms were crossed over his chest, those delicious biceps bulging and visible through his tank. His eyes, a swirling whirlpool of ocean blue, were locked on me, and that steady gaze made me shift in place.

After a bit, the others finally managed to catch on, and once the class's brooms were stable, Coach Heathers bit out, "Mount your brooms." He paused and narrowed his eyes on us, pointing a finger at each of us. "But don't you dare lift off the ground. Those feet better stay on the ground, or I'll pull your bollocks off!"

I did as he instructed, my eyes still on Aidan. The feel of the wood between my legs, barely separated from my core by my shorts and panties, made my mouth part with a small sound. I swallowed and licked my lips as I tried not to be the weirdo getting turned on by the broom. Well, not just the broom. Aidan's heated gaze shared at least half the blame.

Why did just a single look from Aidan get me going? It was as if every blood vessel was on fire, and the only things that could put out those flames were his hands. His large, powerful hands. Fuck! I wasn't sixteen anymore. I'd had sex, with several people for that matter.

"But not Aidan," a little voice whispered in my head.

I was turning into a sex-driven ball of hormones like Coach Heathers had claimed, because Aidan was the only one of my boyfriends I hadn't slept with yet. I hadn't had those hands on my hips as he thrust into me or felt his mouth trailing along my chest. My eyes dipped to the front of his gym shorts and widened at the obvious evidence of his arousal.

My face flushed and my eyes darted up to Aidan's once more. His lips curled up wickedly at the corners in a feral sort of smile that made me lightheaded. All I wanted to do was melt into a puddle under that heat.

"Ey!" Coach Heathers shouted at me, his eyes glaring up at me.

Wait, what?

It was then that I noticed my feet were no longer on the ground and neither was I. My fingers gripped my broomstick tightly, my knuckles turning white as I tried not to panic.

I was flying. In the air. On a broom. I'm okay. It's alright. That's what I came here for, right?

Of course, my useless guardian light wasn't doing its job. It just bobbed there like it was having a dandy old day, while I feared for my life.

"Mancaster, get down, you stupid ninny!" Coach Heathers shouted and pointed at the ground as his face quickly turned red. "I said no going above three feet."

"I didn't do it on purpose!" I shook my head and tried to talk with my hands, but then gripped my broom when I realized that letting go wasn't a smart idea. "How do I get down?"

"The same way you got up there, you dummy," Coach Heathers griped, while the others watched on with a mixture of curiosity, horror, and amusement. It didn't matter though. I was getting higher and higher, and I didn't know how to get down, let alone how I got up in the first place.

Why the heck I thought I needed to know how to ride a broom was beyond me. I'd been perfectly fine with walking and driving. I didn't need to ride a broom. What was I thinking? When I wrote my resume to get a job, where would I put it? Under extracurricular activities? Yeah, right next to transfiguration.

"Mancaster, you get your arse down here now!"

I rolled my eyes and snorted at Coach Heathers. Like that was going to make a difference. All it did was make my broom wobble beneath my hands, which made my heart start to race. I swallowed thickly and tried to find Aidan, but my eyes landed on the ground instead.

This was really high. I was really high up. When did I become afraid of heights? I've never been afraid of them before. At amusement parks, I was the first one to get in line for the rollercoasters, higher, faster, more turns. That had been me, every single time.

Except that had been in a harness with certified workers controlling how fast and high I went. Now it was just me and my magic keeping me from falling face first into the ground.

"Calm down, Mancaster," Coach Heathers yelled at me, now upon his own broom. During my moments of panic, he had flown close enough to me to touch. "You have to keep calm or you're going to hurt yourself."

"I'm trying." I gritted my teeth and gripped my broom tighter. If I held it any tighter, I'd break the damn thing in half and then where would I be? Flat as a pancake on the ground, that's where.

"I can't get you down, Mancaster. You have to do it," Coach Heathers growled, letting go of his broom like it was easy as pie and adjusting his baseball cap. "Just focus. You got up here, you can get down."

"Coach." Aidan's voice, like a deep, broody angel, floated up to where we sat in the air. "Let me try."

Coach Heathers glanced down at the ground and then rolled his eyes before he descended back to the ground. I peeked over the side of my broom and watched as Aidan spoke to the coach for a moment, before preparing to get on his broom. I didn't get the chance to see him get off the ground because my world tipped over at that moment, and I was falling.

I let out a scream that hurt my ears as my hands grabbed for something, anything to hold on to. Thankfully, they grabbed the broom. The wood bit into my palms, and I managed to find every splinter on the shaft in the process. To top it all off, not only was I stuck in the air, but now I was hanging from my broomstick with twenty feet between me and the ground.

Now Aris decided to scream its tinkling sound at me as my legs kicked frantically in midair. I tried to get back up on my broom while it went crazy, dancing in the air around me. Aidan was speaking again but I couldn't hear him through the rush of blood in my ears. My panic had overtaken my good sense, and I knew either my magic or my hands were going to give out soon. That was not going to be pretty.

"Max, let go," Aidan commanded, breaking through my inner turmoil. "Just let go. I'll catch you."

My eyes shot down to where Aidan stood beneath me, his arms out in front of him. I shook my head. "I can't."

"Yes. You can." His gaze softened and he urged me down with his hands. "I've got you. Let go."

I closed my eyes and swallowed hard before taking a deep breath. When I let it out, I uncurled my hands from the broom and prayed to Merlin that I didn't end up on the nine o'clock news. I could just see it now— Half Breed Dies From Broom Mishap - Her Four Boyfriends and Family Mourn.

There was a moment of weightlessness as I fell through the air, and a little yelp escaped my lips in the rush. I prepared myself for impact, my hands going over my head as if it would save me from splattering my brains all over the field. I stopped falling as the warm arms of Aidan surrounded me, and it took me far longer to realize it than I liked to admit.

"I've got you," Aidan murmured in my ear, kissing the side of my head.

My eyes shot open and my hands went around his neck, holding on tight as I realized I hadn't died. Aidan caught me. I was okay. I was okay.

I locked eyes with Aidan, those gorgeous blue orbs that mesmerized me from day one, and smiled. "You caught me," I breathed out, not quite recovered from my fall.

"Always," he responded, holding me to his chest as if he would never let me go. A part of me hoped he wouldn't.

"Eh, well, you look alright." Coach Heathers pulled off his baseball cap and scratched his head before gesturing it toward the school. "Templar, take her to the medics to be checked out just to be sure. And Mancaster..." Aidan turned me to face the coach. "I'll let you off with a warning this time, but next time, you're out of here."

I pressed my lips into a tight line and nodded. "Got it."

Chapter 5

AIDAN AND I ENTERED the medical center with me still wrapped up in his arms. The head healer took one look at Aidan and me, and arched a brow.

"Broom class," I murmured as my face heated up.

"Put her over there." The healer was a large, dark-skinned woman with puffy lips. She seemed to permanently purse them as if she wasn't impressed with anyone or anything. Her name tag read Viola.

Aidan sat me on one of the many beds but didn't leave. Viola gave him a look but didn't say anything as he took a seat in one of the metal chairs next to the bed. I gave him a small smile, thankful to have him here with me.

"Where does it hurt?" Viola asked as she held up her hand. It started to glow a faint yellow light along the surface of her skin. She held it toward me, and I braced myself for... something. I didn't really know what. I'd never been to the healers before. Sure, I'd helped the Headmaster's daughter, but that had been different. It'd been me healing her, not the other way around. For all I knew, healing magic would tickle.

Strangely enough, it didn't tickle... or hurt, for that matter. It was actually pleasant, like taking a warm bath to soothe your aching muscles. In my case, I had plenty of aches that needed to be soothed, but none of them were physical.

"I'm actually fine," I tried to tell her as my mouth twisted into a grimace. "I just had a little fall, but Aidan caught me." I flashed a smile toward the gamer and took his hand. Squeezing it lovingly, I turned back to Viola. "I don't hurt anywhere, I swear."

Viola clicked her tongue and zipped those sharp eyes across Aidan and me. "Fine, but I don't want Coach Heathers in here, yelling and carrying on in my office because I didn't do my due diligence. So, you're going to let me check you over and then you can be on your way."

I huffed and let her get to it.

While Viola scanned her palm over every inch of me... and I mean every inch, inches that not even my parents had gotten close to since I was in diapers... I watched Aidan. His brows were drawn close together, his lips pinched tight as he watched Viola work. He was either having a dude moment where it looked like he was interested in something while really thinking about his car or whatnot, or Aidan was genuinely interested in Viola's work.

"Hey." I grasped his hand a bit tighter, pulling his attention to me. "You never told me what you plan on doing after graduation. It's not that far off, you know."

Aidan blinked at me for a moment and then answered, as he did everything, in as few words as possible. "An apothecary."

"Huh?" My nose scrunched up. "You mean like a pharmacist?"

"Not quite." Viola snorted. "An apothecary does a lot more than those human pill pushers do. They not only mix their own medication, but they can also treat those who are ill." She met Aidan's gaze as she finished up with me. "It takes patience and a deft hand to be an apothecary. Think you're up to it?"

Aidan's chest puffed out as he leveled a confident look at Viola. "Yes."

Viola nodded. "Good. We could use a few more good ones." With that, she looked toward me, then jerked her head toward the door. "You're done. Nothing broken. No internal injuries. You're lucky this one was here to catch you, or we'd be having a very different conversation."

My nose wrinkled at the thought. I knew exactly what she meant. The image of me flat as a pancake on the field was still very clear in my mind. I didn't know if I could get back on that broom any time soon. Except, if I didn't then I would fail the class. Was my sanity really worth it?

"Thank you." Aidan stood and, still holding my hand, urged me to my feet. He slid one large palm along my lower back to support me. His simple touch made my skin feel tight, and suddenly, I was back on the field, wanting those hands touching me in all the right places.

Viola made a noncommittal sound before spinning on her heel to attend to the others in the center. Aidan ushered us out of the office and back toward the way we came. I dug in my heels after a few moments, giving him the choice of stopping or forcing me to move. When he stopped and gave me a worried frown, I shifted so I faced him.

"I don't want to go back to class." I swallowed, and my eyes flicked toward the way we came and then back to him. "Not today." I let out a nervous laugh and tugged on my ponytail. "I think I've had enough flying lessons today."

Aidan didn't argue. He simply nodded as his eyes softened.

We stood there for a moment, not quite awkwardly but not quite knowing what to do next. My stomach, thankfully, answered that question for me as it growled and demanded food. I gave an embarrassed grin as Aidan's lip tipped up at the edges.

"Guess that means it's time for food." I shifted from one foot to the other, chewing on my lower lip. "Do you want to come get something with me? I mean, you don't have to go back and help Coach Heathers, do you?"

Shaking his head, Aidan said in that low, spine warming voice of his, "No, I had a free period and volunteered. He won't miss me."

"Really?" I gaped and then clamped my mouth shut. "I mean, good. Uh. Well, let's go."

I slid my hand into his large one and we walked down the hallway together. It was a companionable silence, one that was neither weird nor uncomfortable. I didn't feel the need to fill the air between us with words, but at the same time, I decided to make more of an effort to get to know Aidan, and that was what I was going to do.

"What's your favorite color?"

Aidan arched a brow and I flushed.

"I mean," I stumbled over my words and wet my lips, "I want to know more about you."

Amusement filled Aidan's blue eyes before they turned back toward the cafeteria. "And you'll know this by knowing my favorite color?"

I winced. "Well, when you say it that way, it does sound silly, but I stand by my choice. One step at a time." I took an exaggerated step forward to prove my point and grinned back at him as he stopped behind me. Aidan gave me one of his rare smiles that had my knees threatening to collapse beneath me, before he reached out with his empty hand to stroke the side of my face.

"Blue," he said as he stared into my eyes.

My whole body lit on fire at that one word and I fell a bit more in love with him. Wait, love? When did that happen? Not that I didn't care for Aidan, I cared about all of them, but love wasn't something I'd thought about since my ex. Aidan was leagues ahead of Jerron though. They weren't even on the same planet as each other.

"Fuck." I shook my head and then grinned up at him. "You just had to be a romantic, didn't you?"

Aidan's brows lifted at my words but didn't respond.

Still grinning like an idiot, I tugged on his hand. "Come on, let's get some food before I end up molesting you right here. I already got in trouble for it once this week, and twice is probably pushing it."

"Twice?" Aidan drawled out as we continued on toward the cafeteria.

I flushed hotly as I cleared my throat. "Uh, yeah. With Dale. Don't ask."

I shook my head and sighed happily when we finally made it to the cafeteria doors. Since it was between meals, there weren't a ton of students in line, so Aidan and I breezed through. I grabbed an apple and carton of milk while Aidan piled a plate full of leftover spaghetti from lunch.

"Geez, hungry?" I asked with a grin.

Aidan glanced down at his plate and then over to me before gesturing to his large form.

"I could see how you need to eat." I nodded. "You're a growing boy after all," I teased and barely got away before his searching fingers jabbed my side. "I'm just saying." I paused to pay for my food and waited for him to do the same. "I don't know where you pack it all away. If I ate like you, I'd be as big as a house."

Aidan snorted and led me to a table.

"I'm serious." I poked his bulging bicep. "You're packing some serious heat in these guns, and I have to say I'm a bit envious. I want to be all hard and muscly."

Pausing mid-bite, Aidan let his eyes drift over my form. The heat in that gaze made my mouth go dry, so I quickly took a drink of my milk.

"No."

"No?" I raised a brow. "No what?"

Swallowing the food in his mouth, Aidan reached out, quick as lightning, and pulled me into his lap. He held me close as one hand trailed up and down my thigh.

"You're perfect," he proclaimed.

I blushed and wrapped my arms around his neck. "Thanks... I think. And I was just teasing. I wouldn't want to be this hard." I shifted in his lap as something beneath me twitched and thickened. I gasped and met his hooded eyes. "I mean, it just wouldn't work," I continued, my mouth moving faster than my brain. "If we were both all muscle and bones, it wouldn't be very comfortable to..." I trailed off and swallowed hard. "You know."

Aidan cupped the back of my neck as the side of his lips pulled up into a grin. "Tell me."

Fuck. Gah, he wanted me to say it. We were in the middle of the cafeteria, I was sitting in Aidan's lap—where he was very happy to have me, by the way—and about two seconds away from foreplay. Of course, no one around us even cared what we were doing. They were too busy trying to study or socialize to pay much mind to the couple being too touchy in public.

I took a deep breath to try to calm myself. Big mistake, it only caused me to inhale Aidan's wonderfully masculine scent, which in turn made my panties become increasingly uncomfortable. I opened my mouth to say that one word, with only three letters, that I'd had more than enough of lately to be able to talk about, let alone just say the damn word, but before I could get it out a commotion from the courtyard had the whole cafeteria looking.

"What was that?" I perked up, taking any chance of distraction from the embarrassingly hot conversation. Aidan didn't answer in words, but he did slide me off his lap, depositing my feet on the floor before standing himself. We followed the few dozen students out into the courtyard greenery to see what had drawn our attention.

Several buses, not big yellow school buses but full-sized charter buses, filled the U-shaped driveway. Why they were parking here and not across the way where the rest of us had to park our cars, I didn't know, but the side of each bus had a different school's emblem on it, which increased my interest tenfold.

The first bus, the color of freshly poured cream, had a crest made up of pale bluebonnets and a large cauldron. The doors to the bus opened and out came a gaggle—or maybe a giggle?—of women. They were of college age, ranging from eighteen to almost thirty, but they weren't dressed like the rest of us here at Winchester Academy.

If I had to describe them, I'd say they weren't simply women, but ladies. Their hair was coiffed and curled, pinned to their heads and covered by small and stylish hats, while their perfectly formed bodies were covered in prim and proper dresses of pale pinks, yellows, and other flowery colors. The clothes followed their curves as if each dress had been exactingly tailored to their forms. Their skirts fluttered around their legs to show off classy matching heels.

"Bluebonnet Academy," Aidan told me from my left. He nodded toward the bus and the ladies looking around like they had stepped into a swamp rather than our campus. "They're from Texas."

I cocked my head to the side. "How do you know that?"

Aidan crossed his arms over his chest, his eyes scanning over the other students pouring out of their buses. "We played them last year."

"Hold up." I held my hand up and turned to him. "You guys had the Games last year and I didn't know about it? How is that possible?"

Aidan lifted and dropped a shoulder. "You were busy."

"I wouldn't think I was so busy that I'd miss something like this." I shook my head as I watched the next bus, a dark tan colored monstrosity with an emblem of a mountain and a spell book on the side, I tried to think about what I'd been doing during my first year here.

Now that I thought back on it, I'd been so focused on trying to get through classes and the awe of it all, that I guess I hadn't really paid much attention to anything else. Oh, and of course there were the guys and then Sabrina trying to thwart me at every turn. None of that would have helped. Plus, my grandparents were on my case every single week about some bullshit or other.

But to be so self-absorbed that I missed a whole grand event like these games? I called foul.

Aidan must have sensed my displeasure and bumped me with his arm, which knocked me over. His hand grabbed my elbow before I could face-plant. A chagrined smile crept up his lips as he smoothed his hands over my arms before leaning down to me.

"Don't feel too bad. It wasn't at our school last year. Every year a school hosts the games. This year is Winchester Academy's turn. They'll be here the whole year." He paused and seemed to think about it before adding, "It's a great honor."

"But still..." My eyes trailed over to the tan bus as the doors finally opened.

"They're from Colorado. The Mountaineers," Aidan informed me as a mixed group of guys and girls came off the bus. They wore jeans, t-shirts, and baseball caps, a lot more... normal than the first team. At least they didn't look too stuck up, not like the Texas Bluebonnets.

"Did you participate last year?" I asked, trying to get a better look. The Mountaineers were a lot more boisterous and ready to play than the Texans... and there was still another bus that hadn't unloaded yet.

"Yes."

I turned my eyes from the avocado bus to look at him. "And I missed that too, huh?"

Aidan shrugged. "We weren't dating then. And I only went for the games. I didn't stay. Too much work here."

"Still, I feel like a right bitch." I sighed heavily. "I should know more about you guys than I do."

A familiar snort came from my right, and I twisted around just in time to see Sabrina flip her long, blonde hair over a shoulder as she walked up. "Well, there are four of them. I'm surprised you keep their names straight."

I wrinkled my nose at her. "It's not hard. They're all different."

Aidan looked softly down at me and I winked at him.

Sabrina shook her head, crossing her pale arms over her pink t-shirt dress. The bangles on her wrist clinked together and shone in the light. "Still, I don't know how you remember who's fucking you, let alone what their favorite color is. Paul's is blue, by the way, and Ian's is green." She gave me a smug grin before flicking her eyes over to the buses. "Ugh, gross. I hate Cali guys even more than the girls. It's always 'bro this, bro that, let's get some grub and smash.'"

I glanced back at the green bus and noticed the wave-and-broomstick crest on the side. The group on the bus had already climbed out and were milling about the side of the bus. The guys among them wore board shorts and tank tops, and most of them had shells on a string around their neck. The girls wore short shorts and bikini tops underneath their shirts. Their tanned skin and sun-kissed hair made me feel lackluster and frumpy. I should go to the beach more.

The thought actually made me wonder what the guys would be like at the beach. I'd have to make a point for us to go together sometime.

"Smash?" I asked Sabrina at last, pulling my eyes away from the group and back to her.

Sabrina's nose curled up in a sneer. "You know, smash? Hit the waves, but unlike those puny humans, they're riding brooms. Fucking jerks don't care who they might expose with their crap."

"Ah, Craftsman, don't be like that, you know we use a concealment charm," a tall, sun-kissed god said as he appeared out of nowhere to throw his arm around Sabrina's shoulders.

"Ew, Chad. Get off." Sabrina shoved his arm off of her like it was something from the bottom of the trash can, not something belonging to a hot guy.

'Chad' flashed us a toothy grin that complimented his bright green eyes. His brown hair was wind tossed, and long enough to brush his ears and nape of his neck. From the shells around his neck, and the red and white board shorts he wore, I could easily guess where he was from. The California wizard arched a brow at me as if making a point to say he knew I was looking and didn't care, before holding a hand out to me.

"Chadwick Von Wooden. And you are?"

Before I could answer him, Aidan stepped closer and put his arm around my waist aggressively. "Taken."

"Whoa, dude." Chadwick held his hands up, giving an easygoing grin. "Just saying hello. I'm not scamming on your girl."

Sabrina scoffed and muttered, "Not yet."

That sounded like it came from experience. I tucked that bit of information away for later and lifted my chin toward Chad. "Max. I'm assuming you know Sabrina and Aidan?" I wrapped my arm around Aidan's waist, hugging him tight to show him I wasn't into the guy before us.

"Yeah, we've met." Chad grinned at Aidan who was still glowering at the wizard. "I didn't know you had a girlfriend though, good for you man."

Just then, Paul and Ian jogged toward us, excitement bright in their eyes. Before I could say anything, Ian pulled me from Aidan's arms, lifted me up, and kissed me right on the mouth. I should have tried not to make a fuss, especially in front of other schools with the potential for drama I didn't need, but my guys had a way of making me forget that I was in a crowd of people. My fingers tangled in his hair as I slanted my mouth over his, letting him fuck my mouth the way he'd done just the other day. When he released me, my lips felt swollen, and my cheeks hot.

Paul, not to be outdone by his brother, scooped me up next, but this time, he dipped me like they did in the movies. He kissed me until I was panting and wanting nothing more than to hole up in my room with the three of them.

"Hold up, hold up. Time out, dude." Chad held his hands up in a t-shape and then whipped a finger to Aidan, and then back to the brothers and me. "I thought she was your girl? Why are they macking on her?"

Aidan didn't answer him, but Ian saw the California wizard and grinned. "Chad, my man! How are those waves back in Cali?" He and Chad shook hands and did some weird bro handshake, while Chad still watched us with his mouth agape.

"They're good. What are you up to?" Chad's eyes finally left my flushed face and went to Ian, who didn't seem to care what the guy thought.

"Good." Ian slipped an arm around my waist while Paul held my hand. "I see you've met my girlfriend, Max."

"Your girlfriend?" Chad's brows went up another notch then shot a wary look at Aidan. "I thought she was yours?"

Sabrina took this moment to insert herself into the conversation again with a wicked grin. "Oh, didn't you hear? Max is the new queen witch now and has gathered herself quite a little group of groupies."

I scowled at her. "They're not groupies."

"Whatever." Sabrina shrugged and stared at her nails. "You fuck them all, and they do what you want, so if that's not a groupie, I don't know what it is."

"It's called a relationship," I snapped back. "And I thought you weren't going to be a bitch this year?"

Sabrina arched a perfectly manicured brow. "When did I promise that?"

Before I could answer, a high-pitched squeal permeated the air, which made most of us wince... but made Sabrina's face scrunched together in a snarl. We turned to see one of the Texan ladies heading our way with a jubilant expression on her face. Red curls flowed down her back, her piercing green eyes alight with joy while the mint green dress floated around her form. Two other ladies flanked her, one with blonde hair cut short and dressed in a sunflower yellow dress, and the other with dark hair and a violet colored dress.

"Sabrina, darling!" The redhead opened her arms as she came toward us.

"Oh, fuck," Sabrina muttered, visibly flinching before the redhead even hugged her. "I change my mind, there's something I hate more."

Chapter 6

"MY WORD, AREN'T YOU a sight for sore eyes?" the red bombshell crooned in her Southern Belle accent, a voice that had several male and female students alike turning their heads as she embraced Sabrina.

The blonde in question hid her snarl behind a smile that even I could tell was fake. "Beth Ann, how lovely to see you again. Has it been a year already?" Sarcasm filled Sabrina's voice as she pulled away from the hug as soon as she could.

Beth Ann giggled politely and fluttered her long lashes as if she were waiting for someone to bring out cameras and start a photo shoot for her at any moment. "Oh, darlin', I don't know how y'all can handle this Georgia weather, it's killer on my curls. Back home, at least it's a dry heat." She fanned herself while exchanging a cool smile with her friends who held back to let her take point.

"Well, we like it just fine," Ian shot back, pulling the redhead's attention our way. "Perhaps you should go home then."

Those bright green eyes slid over Ian and Paul appreciatively, moving right on over me like I wasn't even between the two brothers. A slow satisfied grin, like a cat who'd had too much cream, crept up her face.

"Why, Ian Broomstein, as I live and breathe! I didn't know you were still walking the halls of Winchester Academy. You don't write, don't call…" She pouted and stepped a few paces closer so she could place her hand on the arm not wrapped around my waist. "I was beginning to think you forgot about me and that long winter break we spent cuddled up in my daddy's cabin."

My heart pounded in my chest and my stomach twisted into knots at the blatant way Beth Ann was coming on to Ian right in front of me. Geez, was I invisible or what?

I had thought all the mean girl antics were over with Sabrina now ostensibly a friend, but it seemed that I was just trading up for a newer, more primped-up model of bitch. At least Sabrina acted like she lived in our century and not like she was the star in some *Gone with the Wind* remake.

Thankfully, Ian wasn't playing Beth Ann's games. His arm tightened around my waist as he stiffened against her touch. "I had, actually." Instead of giving into her not-so-subtle hints, Ian pulled me a bit closer to his side. "Have you met my girlfriend, Maxine Mancaster?"

Beth Ann's sultry gaze slipped over to me, surveying every inch of me as she glanced up and down my form. Whatever she saw, she clearly didn't find me worth her time, but she hid any venom in her eyes quickly behind a smile even faker than Sabrina's.

"Beth Ann Scarlette." She offered me one of her pale tiny hands, slipping a sly grin over her shoulder at her friends who had matching expressions. "Of the bourbon Scarlettes."

"I don't know who or what that is, but I'm Max." Against my better judgment, I took the hand she offered and gave it one firm shake before trying to take it back. Beth Ann, however, had an inner strength hidden under all that simpering lady facade and held on tight.

"These are my closest friends in the whole wide world, Bridget and Abigail." She gestured to the blonde and then the brunette respectively. "You're a Mancaster? I heard that right?" She angled her head toward Ian, but kept her gaze on me.

My brows bunched together as I narrowed my eyes on her. "Yes, I am."

She hummed and then a wicked smile curled up her lips. "I wasn't aware that Nina and Harold had any children. Last I heard, they had disowned their only daughter for marrying a human." She let out a small laugh.

While I didn't like where she was going with this, I wouldn't back down. I stepped out of Ian and Paul's arms, something that Beth Ann definitely took note of, and into her personal space.

"Yes. My mom is Peggy and my dad, Wesley, is human. Do you have a problem with that?"

Beth Ann stared at me for a moment, then she covered her mouth with the back of her hand and let out an annoying laugh. "Oh, my, you are something else, aren't you?"

"She sure is," Paul drawled, and pulled me back to lean against his front. "There's not another girl like her."

I sighed into his embrace, a warmth filling my heart as I suddenly didn't give two rats' asses about Beth Ann or her time with Ian at her 'daddy's' cabin. I was with them now, and that was all that mattered.

Beth Ann's eyes flitted between us and then over to Ian, a frown pulling at the edges of her lips. Then her searching eyes moved to Aidan and that simpering smile came back in full force. "Why, Aidan Templar, look at you all quiet and hiding in the background as usual. Don't you ever get tired of being overlooked?"

Aidan stared at her without bothering to give her an answer.

I didn't like the way she talked about him. Beth Ann acted like she knew my guys and even Sabrina. It made me want to slap that smug expression on her face or maybe find a spur to shove up her annoying ass.

"So, did you guys meet during the last MagiX Games?" I asked as I tried to push back the need for violence and moved my finger around the group. Ian and Paul shifted next to me as if it were something they didn't want to talk about, but Beth Ann seemed more than happy to fill in the blanks.

"Oh, we go way back. Don't we, darlin'?" She directed that sultry purr in Ian's direction. Ian gave a weak nod but let her continue to answer for them. "You see, before we all went off to our respective colleges of choice..." Beth Ann paused and giggled. "Well, our parents' choice anyway, we all went to summer camp together, Camp Merlin."

She sighed a bit dreamily and her friends echoed her sentiment. "It was like nothing else y'all'd ever been to before. Every day was like a dream come true, especially when I had this handsome gentleman just waiting to steal my heart and," she gave Ian a coy smile, "any other part of me he could get those naughty hands on."

"I don't remember you complaining," Ian retorted as he tucked his hands in his pockets with a frown.

"Who would?" Beth Ann winked in my direction, and then turned her eyes on Sabrina. "I hear you have had a taste of our bad boy Broomstein as well. Can't say that I blame you, one brother is good, but two?" She gave a little shrug and grinned. "Who could resist?"

Sabrina gritted her teeth as her hands curled into tight fists. I felt bad for her. I mean, I shouldn't because Sabrina had done the exact same thing to me not too long ago, but having been on the receiving end of such nastiness, I wanted to protect the blonde who was now two seconds away from pulling Beth Ann's red hair out of her head.

"But as I was saying, it feels good to have us all together again." Beth Ann beamed, her hands clasped in front of her and her shoulders up to her ears. "Of course, y'all never could beat my team at camp, so I doubt y'all will do much better against me and my ladies this time around."

"Now, now, hold up." Ian held his hands up, an arrogant grin on his lips. "You only won then because I went easy on you."

"Ha, you wish!" She shoved a finger at him with an arched brow. "You just can't admit that I'm better than you."

My lips pressed into a hard, thin line as I watched them interact so easily. Ian had been standoffish to her so far, but now that they had something to discuss that he cared about, it seemed like that cold mask he'd put up was cracking. I wasn't sure how I felt about that.

I mean, I didn't want to be that jealous girlfriend. I also wasn't sure if I was allowed to be. I was dating all four of them, and of course we'd talked about being exclusive to just me, but I wasn't sure if that was fair.

Paul squeezed my shoulders, massaging them as if he knew I needed some reassurance. However, while I was worried about Ian's reaction to Beth Ann, they were really getting into it and now Sabrina had joined in.

"Forget it." Sabrina shook her head, a mean glint in her eyes. "There's no way… no way… that the Bluebonnets win this year. Winchester will take home the trophy for sure."

"Oh, really, little witch!" Beth Ann smirked and flipped her hair over her shoulder. "Then put your magic where your mouth is." She pursed her lips and looked Sabrina up and down. "Or are you a yellow belly 'possum?"

Sabrina gasped. "I am not and you're on. Winchester versus Bluebell." She held her hand out to Beth Ann with a gleam in her eye that would have made the Devil shake in his boots.

"Same terms as usual?" Beth Ann asked before shaking Sabrina's hand.

"You got it," Sabrina quipped back, and then released her hand with a jerk.

"What are the usual terms?" I whispered to Ian but he waved me off.

"Don't worry about it."

But I did want to worry about it. I didn't trust Beth Ann or Sabrina as far as I could throw them, especially not this new witch. I'd rather go up against the witch I knew than the witch I didn't, and right now, they were both up to no good.

Beth Ann turned away from Sabrina to smile sweetly at Ian, but when she saw me clutching his arm, my front pressed against him with Paul up against my back, she paused and frowned again. She opened her mouth, probably to say something nasty, when Chad reminded us all that he was still here.

"Beth Ann, man, you're really just gonna ignore me like that." Chad grabbed her around the waist and pulled her into a huge hug that had Beth Ann screeching.

"Put me down, you sand sniffin' bum. Now." She smacked at his shoulders while the rest of us laughed at her.

Chad did as she asked, but not before spinning her around several times so fast that it even had me dizzy. When he sat her down, her hands came up to her face and hair, trying and failing to fix what the wind had done to her effortless look. Now, she resembled something close to a hedgehog with the way her hair was sticking out all over the place, and her little hat had come unhooked so that it was now hanging halfway down her curls.

Her friends quickly came to her rescue, trying to help her put herself back together, but Beth Ann either was used to their fussing or didn't care because she glared at Chad as if they weren't there.

"How dare you touch me?" she chided. "Just because we're engaged does not mean you have any right to manhandle me."

"Engaged?" Sabrina's brows lifted, and then a gleeful expression covered her face. "Why, I didn't know you two were in love!"

"We're not," Beth Ann snapped, adjusting her dress before she let out a huff. "Our parents made the arrangement, and while I had hoped to convince a certain wizard to change his mind..." She gave Ian a side-eyed glance that none of us missed. "They were impatient to find me a match before graduation. Chadwick was my second choice."

Chad winked and kissed the air in Beth Ann's direction. "Love you too, babe."

The expression on her face looked like she had swallowed something vile, but I was too lost in my own thoughts about the whole mess. I just couldn't understand it. Why marry someone you can't stand? What was the point in it? We were in the modern era, weren't things like that unheard of now?

Then again, Paul and Sabrina's parents had wanted them to get married too, so I supposed it wasn't too out there, but at least they seemed to have liked each other at one point. Beth Ann seemed like she would rather stab herself in the eye with a fork than marry Chadwick. The fiancé in question didn't seem to care one way or the other, but then again, it might just be the laid back persona he was putting on in public. Behind closed doors, he might be a completely different person.

"Well," Paul interrupted, changing the topic, "I'm happy we're hosting the games this year. It's hard to get away from our studies to travel every year. I hope that I get to have a chance to compete against you all."

Ever the team player, Paul beamed at the others like we were discussing the weather and not a big sporting event. When I had first heard about the event, I went to the library and scoured for everything I could read on it. But like most sports, you couldn't just learn from the books. I wouldn't *know* know about it like they did until I actually went to the games. Or preferably competed in them.

What I did know was that it had started around the time the Olympics had and with the humans having their own sporting competition the magical world felt they couldn't be one-upped and started their own.

"I can't wait until next year." Sabrina sighed, popping one hip out as she fidgeted with her nails. "The international games are so much more fun than these kiddie ones we have here. Plus, who doesn't want to go shopping in France?" Her eyes lit up, and her mouth spread into a wide, toothy grin.

Beth Ann shrugged a shoulder, not particularly excited. "We go to France every summer, don't we ladies?"

Sabrina turned her eyes to me and arched a brow. "Have you been to France?"

"I haven't been anywhere outside of the United States." I shook my head. "I haven't even left Georgia, except for the one time I went to tour Brown University."

"Aw, you poor dear," Beth Ann and her friends cooed in unison as she reached a hand out to touch my arm. "Y'all'd think with all your family money, ya'll'd be able to afford to travel, but then again, it's your grandparents that have it all, isn't it?" She paused and then moved in close. "Enjoy the freedom you have now because once you enter our world, you'll find that what you want," her eyes flicked over to Ian and then back to me, "doesn't matter." Like a switch being flipped, her expression changed to a chipper one, and she waved with her fingers. "Tootles."

When she whipped around, her hair almost smacked me in the face as she sashayed away. The tension around us seemed to melt away the farther she walked. It certainly did for Ian as well.

I watched him out of the corner of my eye, searching for any longing he might have had for her. She clearly still had a desire for him, that was plain in Beth Ann's face whenever she looked at him, but Ian wasn't even glancing her way. He was talking to Aidan in low tones about something to do with Potion Ball, which reminded me...

"Hey, weren't you going to gear me up for Potion Ball and teach me how to shoot?" I slipped out of Paul's arms and shifted between the other two men. "I mean, now's as good a time as any, right? Besides, this whole bet thing is making me antsy to get in some target practice." I mocked shooting a gun at the back of Beth Ann's head from across the way and laughed.

The others laughed with me, and Aidan took my hand, pulling me closer so he could press a kiss to my forehead. "Whatever you want."

"Well, then," I beamed up at him, "I want to learn how to shoot because I have a sudden need to blow something up."

Ian threw his head back and laughed. "Okay, hold on there, Rambo. Let's start with something small first, like some regular paintballs. Then we can work our way up to potions, but first," his gaze slid provocatively over my form as his hands came to settle on my hips, "we have to get you out of these clothes..."

I gaped at him as my body screamed yes, yes, yes!

"... and into some gear," Ian continued. I laughed and smacked his chest as he winked at me. "But I wouldn't say no to some naked fun time later."

I cupped his face with my hand and pushed up on my toes as if I was about to kiss him, but stopped just a hairsbreadth away. "Only if you can beat me."

Ian grabbed me by the back of the neck and closed the distance between us with a toe-curling kiss. When he released me, he smirked.

"I'll take that bet."

Chapter 7

UNFORTUNATELY, I STILL HAD classes to attend before I could get outfitted for Potion Ball. I had to say, that day in Political Studies of Magick, I didn't hear a word the professor said. I was too excited about shooting a gun for the first time.

Okay, so I'm not one of those people who approved of having guns in your house. My mom and dad never owned one, and so I figured I didn't need one either. However, thinking back to it now, having a gun in our house when my mom was a badass witch seemed a bit redundant. Even hilarious.

Could you imagine?

Someone breaks into our house and my mom goes for the gun rather than snapping her fingers and making them forget what they were doing in the first place. Or even worse, snapping your fingers and they're in their underwear in the middle of the police station with a sign around their neck saying, 'I'm a thieving bastard, arrest me.'

Okay, okay. So that last one was a bit farfetched but still, a girl could daydream.

And I was. Daydreaming that is. About guns. Potion Ball guns. I wondered if they were anything like paintball guns, not that I'd ever used one of those either. I did do a quick online search for paintball guns. What came back was so much information I didn't know what to keep and what to throw away. What I did get from it was that getting hit by one of those little balls of paint without protection hurt like a bitch. So, that was my main goal now. Don't get hit. Easy enough, right?

"Hey," I grinned and waved at Aidan who waited in the quad for me after class.

Aidan had changed into a pair of black cargo pants and a long-sleeved, skintight shirt, showing off all of those rippling muscles and making my knees feel like jelly beneath me. Over his shirt, he had something that looked like a Kevlar vest but with more straps. Aidan had a black gym bag in one of his fingerless-gloved hands that he had sat on the ground when I approached. As I stopped in front of him, I saw he wore a pair of black combat boots that were laced tight and had residue from something pink and green.

"Here." He unzipped the bag and handed me a mask. The mask was hot pink and had a slight visor over the eyes and would cover my mouth and nose with a few slits in the front for breathing.

"What's this for?" I held it in my hands, turning it over. There were so many straps on the back I wasn't sure I could get the thing on my face, let alone get it off by myself.

Aidan's lips quirked up at the side. "To protect that pretty face of yours."

"I know that." I rolled my eyes, blushing at his compliment. "I meant, I thought we were going to go get me some equipment of my own. Where'd you get this from?"

Shifting from one foot to the other, Aidan didn't answer right away. Then without warning, he took it from me and put it back in his bag. "Forget it. We'll get you another one."

"Hey," I argued, trying to grab for it. "I liked it. Why did you take it back?"

Aidan rubbed a hand over the back of his neck and had a guilty look on his face. If I hadn't been so close to him, I wouldn't have caught it when he muttered, "It was my ex's."

My brows lifted and I glanced down to the bag and back to him. "Oh, so?"

Aidan's eyes met mine and his brows furrowed together. "You're not mad?"

For a second, I had to think about why he would think I was mad. It's just a mask. I mean, sure his ex had worn it, but what did that have to do with me now? I wasn't the type of girl who would freak out over something like that. Besides, it wasn't like he was giving me hand-me-down jewelry or something.

I chuckled and shook my head. Which only made Aidan even more confused. Stepping closer to him, I pushed up on my toes and pressed one hand to the side of his face. "I'm not mad. It's just a mask Aidan." I kissed him softly before pulling away. His arms came out and wrapped around my waist.

"You're such a cool girlfriend." His lips curled up in a genuine, rare smile that made my body warm and had my thoughts drifting from Potion Ball. I wanted to see what he had under all these tight-fitting clothes and I wanted it now.

"Sorry I'm late," Ian called out as he jogged toward us, wearing his own outfit similar to Aidan's, except his was tinged green and he had his face mask sitting on top of his head already.

Fuck, if I thought one of them in their gear was hot, two of them was a sensory overload. My mouth watered, my tongue darting out to wet my lips as I eyed the two of them. Ian caught my look and gave me a lopsided grin.

"Keep looking at me like that, lovely, and we won't ever make it to the store, let alone the practice field." Ian moved in close to Aidan and me, tipping my chin up to kiss me thoroughly. I moaned into his mouth, my fingers curling into Aidan's shirt. Aidan's hands pushed me closer so I could feel how hard he was beneath his pants just from watching us kiss.

"Get a room!" someone yelled as they moved past us.

Ian and I parted with a laugh before Ian lifted his bag and brow, gesturing with a thumb behind him. "Ready to go?"

"Yes." I hopped in place. "Show me all that you know. I am ready to learn."

Aidan and Ian exchanged a look before Ian smirked. "Oh, Maxine. There are so many things I would love to say to that but first, let's get you fitted. Then we'll see about letting you play with some balls."

I giggled along with them as we walked out of the quad and toward the parking lot. I had one arm through Aidan's and my free hand in Ian's. It was an interesting sight to see so it wasn't too surprising to see people staring. Well, not as many as usual and the ones who were mainly staring were the students here for the games. I could see them looking at us and then whispering to each other, pointing fingers in our direction.

"Ugh, I thought we were old news." I tightened my grip on both guys and tried to walk faster.

Ian snorted. "We'll always be news. Regardless of who we're dating. It's part of being who we are. Might as well get used to it, Mancaster." Ian bumped his shoulder against mine and winked. "Everything you do will be scrutinized and dissected."

I groaned and threw my head back. "Can't I just be one of those hermit people, who never goes to parties and only shows up for like funerals and the occasional birthday?"

Aidan grunted in response.

Ian laughed and shook his head. "Not if you want to date all of us. Just worrying about your grandparents is one thing, but neither Aidan's nor my parents are that laid back. You should have heard the earful we got after taking you out on a double date."

I frowned at him. I hadn't thought of that. I guess I'd only thought about how my actions would affect me with my family, not really about all of them. I had only met Aidan's parents so far, but from what everyone has said, I should count my blessings the Broomsteins traveled so much for work. I wondered if Dale's parents were that uptight? He wasn't from an elite family, so they didn't care as much about the image aspect of it. Or at least, I hoped not.

While I contemplated a future meeting of the parents, the guys had brought me through the parking lot and up to a large black Jeep with silver rims and a bumper sticker that said 'Wood or Die.' Aidan and Ian threw their bags into the back of the Jeep before Ian opened the passengers side door for me, while Aidan took the driver's seat.

As I slid into my seat, I glanced around the inside of the Jeep. "This is yours?" My fingers moved over the smooth interior and the total lack of a roof. "What do you do if it rains?"

Aidan threw me a sideways smile as he cranked the Jeep. "Put the roof on."

Ian took the backseat up, sitting in the middle so he could lean forward between us. "Plus, don't tell the humans, but Aidan has an anti-rain charm on his Jeep." He reached forward and flicked a medallion hanging from the rearview mirror. It had a man on it dressed in a long robe with water falling around him.

"Weird." I stared at it for a moment until it stopped spinning and then turned to Aidan with a grin. "So, what kind of music do you like?" I didn't wait for him to answer before turning on the radio to see what he had the station set on. Classical music came pouring out of the speakers. I arched a brow at him. "Really?"

Aidan lifted a shoulder. "It's soothing."

I exchanged a look with Ian before flipping the channel to something less headache inducing. "You know, I figured you more for a heavy metal or maybe even grunge kind of guy, not a classical music guy."

While he drove us to where we were going, Aidan gave me a sideways look.

"What?" I lifted a shoulder. "You have that broody suffer in silence look about you. How am I supposed to know what you are like if you don't tell me?"

Ian chuckled and patted me on the shoulder. "Don't worry, we've been friends since elementary school and still I don't know all this guy's deepest and darkest secrets."

"But you can tag team a girl just fine," I pointed out, and flushed as both of them gave me a heated look. Shifting my seat, my panties becoming increasingly more uncomfortable by the minute, I asked, "So, have you done that a lot?"

"Done what?" Ian arched a brow, his lips quirking up at the ends. He was obviously screwing with me. He wasn't that dense. He knew what I was talking about.

I stared hard at him for a moment, waiting for him to give it up, but it seemed like he wasn't going to budge and really wanted to hear me say it. The pervert. "You know, uh." I cleared my throat and ducked my head. "Had a threesome."

Aidan watched me with amusement, while Ian grinned and said, "If you can't say it then you can't do it."

"Not fair." I pointed a finger at him and pouted. "Just because the thought of doing it with both of you at once is hard to verbalize, doesn't mean that I am incapable of doing the actual act."

"And do you?" Ian prodded.

"Do I what?"

Ian inclined his head with eagerness in his eyes. "Want to have a threesome with us?"

My brows furrowed. "Didn't I already do that before?"

Ian shook his head. "Not really, not with Aidan."

"Oh." My eyes shifted to the quiet man and lingered on him. I wondered what was going through his head right now. Did he want to have a threesome? Was that something he enjoyed? We hadn't quite gotten to the point where we'd had physical sex in the way that Ian was talking about. Aidan and I'd done a lot of foreplay and flirting, but not the actual act itself.

I reached over and placed my hand on Aidan's leg. He looked away from the road for a moment to meet my gaze. Chewing on my lower lip, I watched his face. Searching for some sign of him wanting to do what Ian had suggested or if he would prefer our first time to be with just one another.

"I just want to be with you." Aidan's low voice moved through me and settled between my thighs, making it unbearably hard to stay in my seat and not jump him right that second. For one, we're in public. For two, moving vehicle. Bad. Bad. I didn't want to die just for an orgasm, but I was sure Aidan could give life-altering ones all on his own.

As we drove, we made idle chitchat about the coming year and the games, but not even talking about what kind of magic I might learn this year could distract me from where we were going. First, to get me some snazzy clothes like them and then I didn't know why, but I was itching to get my hands on one of those guns and shoot something.

"Here we are." Ian smacked the back of my seat, hauling himself up and out of the Jeep before Aidan had even stopped the vehicle.

Aidan and I waited until he parked before a large shop, smack dab in the middle of a sad looking parking lot, with a rundown front. The sign was hanging by a wire and it looked like the place wasn't even open, let alone running anything to do with Potion Ball. Despite its outward appearance, the parking lot had tons of cars in it, making me even more confused.

"Uh, not to be a buzzkill," I started, my nose crinkling up against my face. "But are you sure this is the right place? It's not exactly what I had in mind."

Aidan came around to my side of the car, opening the door with his hand rather than magic. I liked that about him. While he had magic, he didn't use it for frivolous things. He preferred to do them the human way.

Offering me his hand, Aidan gave me a small smile. "You should know better by now."

"What?" I grinned, slipping my hand into his as he pulled me from the Jeep. My front collided with his large chest, making my pulse throb and my mouth go dry.

Ian appeared on the other side of me, his body lining up with my back and his mouth brushing against my ear. "Nothing is what it seems in our world."

I licked my lips and swallowed, more than happy to be sandwiched between the two of them again. With Aidan's hands on my shoulders and Ian's on my hips, I had the urge to wiggle around like a cat, covering them with my scent and reveling in the feel of them.

Unfortunately, at that moment a group of people came out of the unpleasant looking shop, slowing their footsteps as they moved by us. I flushed at the curious looks and stepped out from between the two wizards. Fuck me and my hormones. If it hadn't been for those gawking shoppers, I'd have more than likely let myself do some serious PDA in the middle of the parking lot.

"Uh, so..." I cleared my throat. "About this shop?" I turned toward the building. "Is it spelled or what?"

Ian shoved his hands into his pockets and nodded toward the front door. "Just walk across the threshold and see."

I eyeballed the two of them, neither of whom seemed to be in any hurry to move in that direction, before walking that way. Every step I took toward the shop made my heart beat faster. Excited to see what lay beyond those broken down doors, I hardly noticed the guys slowly following behind me.

When I got to the line of the door, I noticed it—the shimmer of a magical barrier. I shouldn't be so surprised by magic anymore. I'd been in the world long enough that I should be used to it, shouldn't I? Regardless, a giddy feeling overcame me as I took that final step, letting the magic wash over me as I blinked into the shop before me.

The room wasn't dark and dusty like the windows on the outside would have me believe. Inside, there were bright lights, racks of products, clothing, equipment, and people. Lots of people. It reminded me of a Dick's or Bass Pro Shop. Well, if they had brooms that zipped across the room with sale signs hanging down from them. Or Potion Ball guns that demonstrated themselves.

"So..." Ian threw an arm around my shoulders, grinning from ear to ear as he took in the room. "What do you think?"

I giggled and glanced around the room, unable to hold back my excitement. "I think I'm going to get in big trouble when my parents get my credit card bill."

Aidan huffed a laugh, brushing his shoulder against mine as he came to stand beside me. "I'll buy it."

"What?" I gaped at him, shaking my head. "No, no way. I can't. This stuff..." I gestured around the room, my excitement diminishing a little at the thought of how much it would cost me for a whole set of gear. "It's too much."

Ian threw his head back and laughed. "Do you hear her, Aidan?" He turned and pinched my chin between his two fingers, locking his eyes with me. "It seems our girl has forgotten who we are."

Our girl. Oh, those two words made me want to dance and giggle like a schoolgirl. Instead, I cleared my throat and narrowed my eyes on Ian before an idea made my lips curve up into an arrogant smirk. "Who you are?" I leaned in close until our mouths were inches away from each other. "I'm a mother fucking Mancaster. I don't need your money. I've got my own." I sealed the words with a quick kiss before pushing past him and sauntering into the room, fully aware of their eyes on my ass as I left.

Okay, I had no idea how much money my family had—my grandparents had—but from what everyone had been telling me from day one, they weren't hurting for money. In fact, I doubt I would even make a dent in the Mancaster fortune from what I would spend here, and I planned to spend plenty.

I glanced over my shoulder at the two of them, fluttering my eyelashes coyly. "Are you coming, or not?"

Matching heated looks covered both of the wizards' faces, which only deepened at my words. I let my eyes trail over their forms and noticed both had the telltale signs of arousal pushing at their pants. It took everything I had not to gasp at the sight.

Ian and Aidan exchanged a look before they came prowling toward me, with Ian growling out, "Not yet, but I plan to before the end of the night."

Chapter 8

IN THE DRESSING ROOM of the Zelus Magical Sporting Emporium, I shifted from side to side as I stared at the mirror in front of me. The outfit I now wore was one Ian had picked out. It was pinker than pink, and the pants were so tight that my underwear was making a nest in my butthole and digging deeper with every move I made. The top wasn't much better. My boobs were pushed so far up that I could rest my chin on them. Overall, the outfit seemed more for the benefit of the guys than playing Potion Ball.

I stared at my reflection, my nose wrinkling up and my lips turning down as I shook my head. I tried to adjust the top to cover some of my breasts, but that only seemed to make it worse.

"Looks good to me."

My head shot up at the voice as I searched around the dressing room for the owner. I spun around in a circle but didn't see anyone there. Tilting my head back, I looked above in case someone had snuck in that way.

"Over here," the voice said, and I twisted back toward the mirror. My mouth dropped open as I watched my reflection move on its own. One hip popped to the side and the amused curl on my reflection's lips looked way more mature and seductive than it would have ever looked if I had tried to do that myself.

"Uh, you're... you're..."

"You. Duh." My reflection rolled her eyes and then flipped her hair over her shoulder. "Well, the reflection of you. I do have my own thoughts and such... and I think we are looking smokin' hot." She licked her finger and pressed it to her hip. The hissing sound most would have made with their mouths came from a small bit of smoke as if she had put out a fire.

My eyes jumped down to my hip, searching for the reflection of it on myself. I let out a long breath when I realized it wasn't there. I had enough problems as was, and the last thing I needed was a mirror that could make things happen against my will.

"How's it going in there?" Ian's voice called out, jolting me out of my thoughts, and my eyes moved from the mirror to the dressing room door. A second later, his fingers curled over the edge of the curtain covering the entrance, then he pulled it open to reveal Ian leaning against the doorframe, with his arms crossed over his chest as his eyes made a slow perusal of my form.

My skin flushed at the blatant desire in his eyes, his tongue sneaking out to skate across his lower lip, making it shiny and oh so tempting.

"Damn!" My reflection wolf-whistled at Ian, and I shot her a look.

I pointed at the mirror and cocked a brow. "Is that normal?"

Ian looked over my shoulder and smirked. "Oh yeah. All the shops have honesty mirrors. That way you can't blame them for buying something that was clearly wrong for you."

I hummed as my reflection winked at me, her hands on her hips with more attitude than I could have ever mustered.

Ian arched a brow at the mirror, but didn't seem bothered by it at all. Instead, those wicked eyes of his moved back over to me as he shifted away from the door. Ian reached forward and fingered the neckline of the V-neck shirt, his fingertips brushing against my cleavage to leave a hot trail across my skin. "I like this one."

"Of course, you do." I rolled my eyes. "It's more fashionable than practical."

"Slutty Sport," my reflection not-too-helpfully supplied.

I pointed at the mirror. "See? Even she thinks it's stupid." I held my hands out to the side. "I can barely move in this thing without everything popping out, let alone crawl around the woods."

Ian smirked and took me by the hips. "That's alright. You can be there for morale." He wagged his eyebrows suggestively.

I barked a laugh and shoved him back. "Yeah, right. Not happening."

Before Ian could make another lewd suggestion, Aidan appeared in the doorway and threw a shirt and pants over Ian's head. "Here."

I took them from his large hands, and one glance told me that I would like these much better than what Ian had picked out. The top was a lightweight, long-sleeved top with a scoop neck that would settle on my collarbone and not even show a hint of boobage. The pants were looser, more like the cargo pants they were both wearing than the tight yoga pants currently wedged up my butt.

"Thanks." I beamed at Aidan and moved to change, but noticed that Ian wasn't leaving. I pushed him with one hand until he was outside the door.

"Hey!" Ian chuckled and grinned. "I can help."

I pursed my lips and shut the curtain in his face. With my reflection chattering about how I should have let Ian in to do scandalous things to me, things that even made me blush, I quickly changed into the new outfit.

"Now that is kickass." My reflection nodded in approval. "I liked the other one better, but this one... Damn girl, nobody will think about messing with you."

I smirked at my reflection. I did look pretty badass, though the fact that my hair was hanging down around my face annoyed me. I peered into the mirror and cocked my head to the side. I wondered...

With a push of power, my hair lifted into the air and braided into two long braids on either side of my head. My reflection's hair mimicked mine, as well as when I made my slashes of black on each cheek with my magic finger, like they do at football games.

I struck a power pose, fists curled tight as I smirked at myself. "Now I'm ready."

I turned my back on my reflection and pulled the curtain open. Ian and Aidan turned from the gun they were messing, and their eyes landed on me.

"So, what do you think?" I asked.

Aidan nodded appreciatively.

"I liked the other one," Ian started, but then nodded too. "But this one is more you."

I grinned at then both before inclining my head toward the gun in Aidan's hand. "Is that for me?"

"Yes." Aidan held the gun up and out to me. "It's smaller. For your..." He gestured toward my hands.

My heart warmed at his actions. Aidan was so thoughtful and yet so quiet he couldn't put his actions into words.

I took a few steps closer to them and held my hands out to take the gun. It was much lighter than the one Ian had in his room. And unlike the pink monstrosity of the outfit Ian had picked out, this gun had not a hair of that color on it. It was all black and sleek with a hint of silver on the butt, and I liked the weight of it in my hands and tried to imagine myself shooting it.

"Now that's a sight I won't soon forget," a familiar voice came from our right.

All three of us turned to see Dale standing at the edge of the clothing racks. His lips were curved up as his eyes scanned up and down my form.

"Hey, you." I handed the gun to Aidan on my way over to Dale. I practically jumped into his arms, wrapping my legs around his waist as my arms tangled in his hair and my mouth sank onto his.

Dale's hands came up, holding my butt so I didn't slide down, while his mouth opened for me. I groaned and wiggled a bit against him, causing him to grunt.

Pulling back to take a deep breath, I adjusted his glasses on his nose. "Where have you been this week? I haven't seen you since Pottery class."

Ian snorted and muttered, "Pottery."

Dale patted me on the butt then sat me down, shooting Ian a look that clearly said fuck off. "Sorry, I've been busy. Swordson has had me working on the welcoming committee, as well as being a game organizer for this year's MagiX Games." He dragged a hand through his hair with a sigh. "I haven't had time to wipe my own ass, let alone find time to be with you."

"It's okay, I get it." I shifted from side to side, fingering his button-down shirt before I cocked my head to the side. "So, what are you doing here?"

"Yeah, don't you have some out-of-staters to keep happy?" Ian teased as he crossed his arms over his chest. Meanwhile, Aidan was messing with the hopper of the gun, not really seeming to care what we were talking about.

"Unfortunately." Dale's nose crinkled up, and he shoved his glasses up once more, even though they didn't need it. "Some of those students are right pains in the ass."

"And others?" I drawled as the image of the Bluebonnets and how they'd had no problem hitting on someone else's guy came to mind.

Dale seemed to notice my deflation and tugged on one of my braids before pressing his lips to mine. "None of any consequence."

I grinned up at him, biting my lower lip with pleasure. Dale released my braid but didn't stop touching me, his hands settling on my hips. "As well as babysitter and game organizer, I have to make sure we have the supplies we need and that everything is up to regulation. You'd think we'd have people for this." He rolled his eyes as the sarcasm dripped off his words.

"Yeah," Ian scoffed and bumped Dale on the shoulder. "You."

As he shook his head, Dale moved his eyes up and down my form once more. "I don't have to ask what you're doing here. It's clear these two are outfitting you for the games." He held my arms out to the sides to get a good look at me. "I have to say... I don't hate it." Dale winked and gave me a salacious wag of his brows.

My thighs rubbed against each other, trying to quell the need building there from all the guys' attention. Clearing my throat, I jerked my head toward Ian and Aidan.

"They're going to teach me how to play Potion Ball."

"Oh, really?" Dale cocked a brow at the two of them before frowning. "Is that the gun you're getting her?"

"Yes," Aidan answered, holding it out for Dale's inspection.

Dale moved away from me to look at the gun, and I mourned the loss of his attention.

It was quickly replaced with growing interest as I watched Dale pull the gun apart to inspect each component before putting it back together, all within a few seconds. Wow. I'd never thought I'd be someone who'd get turned on by the sight of a guy holding a weapon, but something about Dale standing there, holding that gun and knowing what to do with it, made a shiver of delight run through me.

"It'll do." Dale handed it back to Aidan as he turned back to me. "You want to shoot some targets? They have some practice ones in the back of the store for you to try out the guns." He pointed a finger toward the back.

I followed his finger, looking toward where the store changed from a metal building into a wooden area. Vines and trees grew from the walls and then sprung up as if it were a perfectly normal place to be. Why hadn't I noticed that before? There were people going through the area with their own guns in hand, laughing and ready to try out their new weapons. Some of them had fishing poles, and I couldn't help but wonder what they did, but I tried to stay on track.

"Do you have time to?" I asked Dale, who looked down at the watch on his wrist, his brows drawn together.

"I have a bit of time before Swordson starts blowing up my phone." Dale grinned and took my hand, leading me toward the back of the room.

"Hey!" Ian exclaimed, marching up behind us to break through our hands. "If anyone is teaching her how to shoot, it's Aidan and me. We brought her here."

Dale gave Ian an arrogant grin. "But I'm the better shooter. You wouldn't want our girl to learn from someone who wasn't a sharpshooter, would you?"

Ian gritted his teeth but moved back, allowing Dale to take my hand once more. I grinned up at them all, more than enjoying how they were fighting over teaching me. It made me feel wanted, and I would be lying if I said I didn't enjoy it.

Dale had a smug expression on his face as he moved us through the store. When we came to the end of one of the clothing area, we jumped back before we almost got ran over by some kid racing his friend on one of the brooms.

"Watch it!" Aidan called out, making the kid turn around, his eyes wide with fear at Aidan's imposing form. The kid wasn't watching where he was going and flew right into the ladies' changing room, causing a chorus of screams.

"Poor kid," I mused, trying to see if he was alright.

Ian shook his head and laughed. "Don't worry about him. I'm sure he's more than happy to have run into the arms of a bunch of half-naked women. Come on." He clapped a hand on my shoulder, throwing his arm around my side not occupied by Dale. "Let's go test this thing out before four-eyes gets called back to his master."

Dale glared at Ian. "I'm not his dog, if that's what you're getting at."

"Might as well be," Ian shot back. "The Headmaster has you on a leash, and you might as well admit it. You can't even scratch your balls without his permission."

Dale snorted. "I fuck Max well enough."

"Dale!" I smacked him on the shoulder with a scowl. "This was funny a second ago, but now you're both acting like children." I shifted out of their grasps and moved to stand by Aidan. "Neither of you will show me crap today." I turned to him with a sweet smile. "Aidan, since you're the only one who isn't acting like a hobgoblin, will you teach me?"

Aidan glanced down at me and then, without a word or look at the others, nodded his head once before taking my hand and leading me into the practice area.

Twisting around slightly, I gave Ian and Dale a finger wave. "Better luck next time, boys."

We left the others behind as Aidan led me deep into the practice area and through the throngs of people, until we were at a small space set up a lot like a mundane shooting range with a row of targets near the back, but instead of a wall, there was a shimmering mystical shield surrounding the area. Past that, there was a last line of trees and beyond, I caught sight of the street where cars passed by without a clue.

Dale and Ian hadn't followed us thankfully. I didn't need them bickering in my ear while I tried to learn this game. I had a hard enough time figuring out Monopoly without distractions, let alone magical paintball. Who knew whom I could end up hurting with a stray shot?

As we slowed to a stop before the targets, Aidan held the gun out to me. I took it from his hands then glanced between it, and then half a dozen red and white circles floating in the air at different distances and heights.

"So, what?" I asked curiously. "I just point and shoot?"

Aidan let out a huff that sounded like a cross between a snort and a laugh. "Not yet."

I walked into one of the small series of stalls that separated the shooters testing their purchases, the target range spread out before me as I held the gun in my hands, not quite sure how I was supposed to hold it. Aidan moved up a few steps, looming behind me, as his hard chest pressed against my back and head. Aidan lifted my arms and aligned my body so that I was holding the gun with both hands. My elbows were up midway, and my hips were turned straight with the top half of me slightly twisted. I tried to pay attention to the movements Aidan was trying to show me, but all I could think about was the hard bulge poking me in my lower back.

Was Aidan… Did Aidan get turned on by this? I mean, he was a dude and guys tend to like this kind of stuff, especially when they had a chance to be all masculine and what not, but it was hard to think about the fact that Aidan was getting a hard-on right now. It was kind of making me hot and bothered as well.

"Max?"

"Huh? What?" I blinked rapidly, turning my head to look at Aidan over my shoulder. He arched a brow and looked down at me expectantly. "Sorry." I cringed. "I zoned out."

Aidan inclined his head once before continuing to show me how to stand and aim the gun, his large, warm, rough hands moving over mine as he showed me how to work the safety and squeeze the trigger. Once more, I found myself thinking of the part of him that twitched against my back, and before I knew it, I shifted against it, pushing my hips back toward him.

A small grunt came from Aidan, and his hands fell from my arms to my hips, holding me still. I licked my lips and glanced over at him beneath hooded eyes.

"Um, like this?"

"Yes." Aidan's voice came out a low growl that made my eyes flutter shut for a second. I forced myself to take a breath and open them again.

"Okay, I think I'm ready." Oh, so ready. "Just point at the targets, right?"

Aidan grunted his approval, but didn't move away from me as I lined up the shot with the gun. Before I could pull the trigger, though, Aidan stopped me.

"What now?" I asked. "I thought I was shooting?"

Aidan shook his head and then produced the pink face mask from before. I wrinkled my nose at it but let him put it on my face, his fingers brushing against my skin and head as he adjusted the straps. With my equipment all on, Aidan took his place behind me again as he shifted me back into the proper firing stance. I took aim for the easiest of the targets, one that was only fifty feet away at eye level, and squeezed the trigger.

The shot went a bit to the left, but I hit the target.

"I did it!" I let out a girly squeal and jumped in place until I faced Aidan. "Did you see? I hit the target."

Aidan's lips pulled up at the edges, then he jerked his head toward the other targets. "Again."

A thrill of excitement ran through me as I repositioned myself. Aidan stayed close as always, pressed up against my back, adding a sexy edge to the act of shooting the gun itself. Without stopping, I kept shooting until my hopper was empty and the targets were littered with colored splotches.

My mask fogged up at the edges from my heavy breathing as I turned to face Aidan. He watched me with hooded eyes and a slight curl of his lips. Without a word, I shoved the mask off my face, set the gun on the stall, and wrapped my arms around his neck as I captured his mouth with mine. Aidan's large hands slid beneath my legs and hoisted me up until I was riding his hips, my center rubbing against his hard abs. Groaning as I pressed closer, I opened my mouth and dragged my tongue against Aidan's. As I pulled it into my mouth, I sucked on it until his fingers clenched on my ass and he let out a low rumble.

Our kissing was just short of dry humping, and who knows where it might have gone if we hadn't been interrupted by a shout a few feet away. "Get a room. Geez!"

My face heated up with embarrassment as I released Aidan and dropped my legs back to the ground. "Let's get out of here before we get kicked out for public indecency."

Chapter 9

THERE WAS A WELCOME party for all the newly arrived guests from other schools tonight. If it was a sanctioned school party, I didn't know, but since it was being held in the quad, I had to assume that Headmaster Swordson knew a bit about it.

"Oh. My. God. Maxine!" Callie squealed, grabbing my arm as her head whipped from side to side, taking in all the students around us. "Thank you so much for inviting me tonight. You are a true friend." Her words drew out in a kind of sigh as Callie's eyes lingered on a female student floating above the crowd.

Callie had pulled out all the stops tonight. She wore a hot red dress that clung to her figure as it fell off her shoulders, and she had crimson lips to match. Her dark hair had been curled and pinned up, some of the tendrils falling around her face. Her eyes were lined with eyeliner and mascara, but she'd gone with just a small amount of light brown powder to make sure her lips were the main attraction. She only did that when she was trying to reel in a guy, one that I had no doubt she would find here tonight if she had her way.

While Callie was a vision in red, I had gone a more subtle route. A strapless, pale blue dress caressed my figure, being held up only by my force of will and a sticky spell. The style was all the rage, or so Sabrina said. Yes, she helped me get dressed for tonight. It'd been her idea to use the spell rather than the human way of hoping your boobs were up for the job. It had also been her who had spelled my hair into a perfect waterfall of curls and topped it with a black headband and strappy shoes.

"A witchy *Alice in Wonderland,*" Sabrina had said with a Cheshire cat grin.

As for herself, Sabrina went with a purple shiny tube dress that she had no problem keeping from shooting up to meet in the middle. I shot a look over to where she was holding court among a few of the out-of-staters. Curves like hers were the envy of all the females tonight, and judging by the way the males were taking in her form, I'd say she wouldn't be wearing that dress for long.

"So, where are your boys tonight?" Callie asked as she took a glass of something fizzy and green off a passing tray. "I'm surprised you're here alone with me and not wrapped up in some kind of orgy right now."

I giggled and shook my head as we stopped by the refreshment table. There, someone had sat out snacks and drinks, not the same ones that were being passed around, but still magical all the same. I hesitated before picking up an orange one that didn't look like it was poured in by a radioactive volcano and took a small sip. Orange soda. Awesome.

"So?" Callie nudged me with her elbow, almost making me spill my drink. She gave me an apologetic smile as I shot her an incredulous look.

"Uh, the guys, they're..." I started, taking another drink of my soda, not wanting to admit that I had no idea where any of them were. After our practice session, Aidan and Ian had taken me back to school where they kissed me and said they had to go do something for class. Of course, Dale wasn't around because of his assistant duties, and I haven't seen hide or hair of Paul yet. I'd been waiting for one of them to text me, but didn't want to text them first, in case I came off as clingy.

Funny, right?

I had four boyfriends, and I was worried about being clingy. If I got any less clingy, I'd be on a different continent. I could win the award for the most secure female in all of Winchester Academy.

So, why weren't they here?

"You don't know, do you?" Callie inquired with a small frown. When I didn't answer and swirled my ice in my cup around instead, Callie huffed. "What's the point of having four boyfriends if you can't show them off?"

Preach.

"I mean, where do they get off acting like that?" Callie continued, getting riled up for me. "Here you are, looking absolutely fuckable, and they're nowhere to be found!"

I shook my head and smiled at her. "That's okay. I have you… and Trina. Hey!" I grinned as my roommate came strolling up with Libby, her girlfriend, and one of Sabrina's henchwomen. Well, hench*woman*. Monica hadn't shown her face after this summer, so it was safe to say she wasn't coming back.

They were quite a pair, Trina with her dark hair and skin dressed in a white jumpsuit, and Libby all blonde and pale. Her black dress tight against her skin with small holes cut in the sides. Night and day, but perfect together. Where Trina was boisterous and loud, Libby was quiet and a bit shy without Sabrina around. They were good for one another, and I liked having Libby around, even if she was a bit dense sometimes.

"Whoa, Max!" Trina's brows furrowed in concern, her head moving from side to side.

"You're looking a bit skinny these days. Looks like you lost a few hundred pounds of man meat." She grinned at me as Libby looked confused.

"Honey, Max is a girl."

Trina gave Libby a soft look before kissing her cheek. "I know, baby. I'm talking about the fact that her boyfriends aren't here."

Libby's lips formed an o-shape. "You're right. Did you dump them? Does Sabrina know?"

I shook my head and grinned at them. "No, and no. I'm flying solo tonight it looks like, and I'm fine with it." The three females stared at me hard, and I let out a nervous laugh. "I am. Look, let's go dance."

"Yeah." Callie giggled, looping her arm through mine. "Maybe your hips will send out a siren call and all four of them will come running."

I rolled my eyes but let Callie drag me onto the dance floor. Libby and Trina wrapped their arms around each other, completely engrossed with one another while Callie and I moved to the beat. Someone had spelled the floor to change colors like we were at a disco. Callie and I giggled and jumped trying to match our movements up with the flickering lights on the floor.

Halfway through the third song, a brown-haired guy with shells around his neck, probably from the Cali group, wrapped his arms around Callie's waist. He dipped his head down to whisper in her ear, and Callie's face lit up. She held up a finger to him and then moved out of his hands to come to me.

"Hey, I know you're alone, but this guy, Josh, wants to dance." She watched my face to see if I was upset.

I know she was worried about me. I was alone at a party without any of my boyfriends. Which yes, I was upset about, and while I didn't really want her to leave me to my own devices, I couldn't tell her no. Callie has been trying to find herself a guy for a while now. She especially wanted one from a wizard school. I think she thought it would make her feel closer to my world or something. I'd tried to explain to her that she was my world, but with Callie, when she got an idea in her head, there's no changing it.

Callie wanted a wizard, so that's what Callie would get.

"Go, go." I pushed her toward the Cali guy with a smile. "I'm fine."

"You sure?" She paused and watched me. She was only looking a little anxious to get back to the new hottie on the floor.

"Yes, I swear. Now go before someone else comes and sweeps him up." I gave her another push toward this Josh guy and smacked her on the butt with a laugh.

Callie grinned over her shoulder and gave me a small wave before looping her arms around Josh's neck. They danced so closely together that I wondered if I should throw a condom in her direction. Knowing Callie, she probably had one stashed in her cleavage.

With a sigh, I turned away from them and focused on dancing. I simply listened to the music and tried to get out of my head. The guys had other things to do. That's fine. I'm fine. I was sure they had other things to do. They'd be here if they could be. Besides, it's not like I haven't gone to a party by myself before. I was a strong independent woman, who didn't need no—

"There you are!" Paul's voice called out seconds before his hands slid around my waist.

Thank fucking God.

I opened my eyes and leaned back into Paul's embrace, glancing over my shoulder. "Here I am."

Paul's chocolate brown eyes twinkled back at me in the dim party light. "Were you lonely without me?"

Yes. "No. I entertained myself well enough."

"Really?" Paul's brows shot up to his hairline. "You looked quite miserable from across the quad."

I pouted and grumbled, "Okay, maybe I was a little miserable."

Paul leaned down and brushed his nose along my bare shoulder and up my throat. A shiver ran through me and I tilted my head further to the side for him. His mouth opened to place hot kisses on my skin, neither of us caring that there was a crowd of students around us. The music had changed to a sultry beat that had my hips swiveling against his in a slow dance. I could feel his need pressed into my backside, hot and hard through the thin material of my dress and his pants.

"I need you," Paul murmured into my ear. "Come with me."

I let Paul take my hand and draw me through the crowd. Smiling and feeling a bit naughty, I gave Trina a little wave when we passed her and Libby on the way out of the quad. Paul's grip on my hand tightened as we stumbled into the hallway, both of us laughing and grinning. Paul hurried us down the corridor, our feet the only sound on the tiled floor. Desire pulsed in my veins, and my heart beat an anxious rhythm, knowing what was to come.

Paul glanced over at me, his own eyes full of need, and I wet my mouth.

"Fuck," he cursed. He stopped us abruptly in the hallway and pushed me back up against the wall. Before I could make a sound, he claimed my mouth with a scorching kiss, one hand sliding beneath the hem of my dress to drag my thigh over his hip as he ground against me.

"Uh," I gasped out, bucking my hips in time with his. I was already slick and ready for him, my clit having a pulse of its own as it begged to be touched. The sound of a throat clearing and an awkward giggle pulled our mouths away from each other. A trio of students, a Cali, a Bluebell, and a Winchester student, stood a few feet away from us and stared. Paul offered them a small smile and dropped my leg to the ground.

"Sorry, too much to drink, I think." Paul chuckled, and they responded in kind before hurrying past us to find their own fun. When they were out of sight, I expected Paul to pick up where he left off, but he kissed me on the nose instead of my mouth. "Come on. I might like sharing you with the others, but I don't want the whole student body seeing what's mine."

Mine. I quite liked the sound of that. I was his, and he was mine too.

We were moving again before I had a moment to think about where we were going. My room was the other way, and like his brother's, I'd never been to Paul's room. I wondered if we would remedy that now.

The door Paul opened wasn't his bedroom. It was a utility closet. I giggled as we stumbled in, Paul pulling me into his embrace as his mouth covered mine. I moaned into his mouth, my fingers finding the fabric of his shirt, twisting and pulling at it. I needed skin. I needed flesh. I needed him.

"Merlin, I want you," Paul breathed against my lips, and his hands dipped beneath my dress to seek out my heat. I sucked in a breath when his fingers found my folds through my panties. My hips pushed against his hand, wanting more contact.

Paul shifted my panties aside, his fingers easily finding my aching clit. My hands tightened on his shoulders as my hips bucked against him. I gasped and moaned, my body already burning with want in mere seconds. I released his shoulders and grappled with his belt. I needed to have him inside of me already.

"Not yet," he whispered, his mouth against my ear. "Come for me first."

"I'll come when you're inside of me," I shot back, but the next thing I knew my hands were frozen, and I was unable to move them any farther.

"What are you doing?" I growled at Paul who grinned down at me in the closet's light.

"I said, not yet." Paul's magic gave me a small push until I was backed up against a shelf. I fought against the magical hold on my hands, frustrated that he wouldn't just fuck me already.

Paul didn't pay my growls and curses any mind as he knelt before me on the ground. The fingers between my thighs pulled my panties to the side as Paul dragged one of my legs over his shoulder.

"Now, that's the prettiest sight I've ever seen." Seconds later, Paul's mouth suction cupped around my clit, pulling and teasing it with his lips and teeth.

White-hot need coursed through me. My head fell back, and a sharp gasp escaped from my throat. A strangled cry pulled from me as I cried out his name. "P-Paul."

"Yes?" He shifted away from me to glance up at my face. His chin and mouth were shiny and made my insides clench greedily.

"Don't stop!" I begged, frantic for his mouth to be on me again. I wanted my hands free, but only enough to push his head back where it had been.

Paul gave me a sly grin. "Either you want to talk, or you don't. You can't have it both ways."

I let out a low growl causing him to chuckle. "Don't fuck with me, Broomstein. You won't like—aaahhh!"

Paul sucked hard at my clit to cut off my threats, and without knowing it, my magic cut through his spell and released my hands. I immediately found his hair, my fingers tangling in the long brown locks. This time, I didn't have a chance to demand him to fuck me. Paul lapped and nipped at my center until I was crying out my release, sagging against the shelf.

While I caught my breath, my eyes flicked to the door. "We didn't use a silencing spell."

Paul wiped his mouth off and then smirked. "So?"

"So!" I smacked his chest with a tired grin. "We could have been caught."

"The door's locked, and besides…" Paul caged me in with his arms before leaning his head down to brush his mouth against mine. "I kind of like the idea of people hearing you scream my name."

I snorted. "You're such a guy."

Lifting a shoulder and dropping it, Paul brushed a bit of my hair away from my face. "What can I say, I'm feeling a bit possessive tonight." His hand cupped my chin, and his mouth covered mine in a kiss that matched his words.

I groaned and pushed up on my toes. I wanted more, but just as my hands went back to his pants, the closet door opened to reveal Ian and Aidan blocking out the light.

"Brother, I'm ashamed at you. Trying to hide away Max when I've had a hard-on for her since…" Ian tapped his chin and pretended to think before grinning. "Well, always. I'm always hard for you."

Chapter 10

"YOU'RE NOT COMING IN here," I told Ian and Aidan, as I gently moved out of Paul's embrace. "There's not enough room. Besides, group sex in a closet?" I wrinkled my nose as I glanced around at the buckets and cleaning supplies, I'd been too busy to notice before. "Not gonna happen. I need a bed... and privacy."

Ian cocked a brow. "Anything else, princess?"

I ignored his sarcasm and adjusted my clothes before pushing between the two and out into the hallway. "Where's Dale?"

"Out there playing host, unfortunately." Ian sighed. "Apparently, the Headmaster was called away on some business and has left Dale in charge of handling the welcome back party."

"Hmmm." I tapped my lip with my finger before turning with a wicked grin. "Then I guess we better liberate him, don't you think?"

I started down the hallway, not waiting for the guys to follow. A few more people than before were making their way out of the party in search of somewhere to get it on just like Paul and I had, so it took longer to get back. As I navigated through the crowds on the way to the quad, I could feel the bass of the music along my skin and beneath my feet.

One glance behind me told me all three wizards were trailing after me. None of them fought to be the one at my side, all of them content to watch me search for our fifth member.

It wasn't hard to find Dale. His auburn hair stood out amongst the students, and he was the only hot nerd in the bunch. I found him by the refreshment table, dragging a hand through his already mussed hair like he'd been doing it all night as he adjusted his glasses on his nose. His lips were pinched at the sides as he pretended to be interested in whatever the person in front of him was saying.

Now, how to get him away?

A sly grin curled up my lips as I had an idea.

"Dale!" I cried out, rushing to his side to grip his arm with frantic urgency. "There you are! We have a problem. You have to come now."

Dale's green eyes moved to me and widened with concern. "Max? What is it? Is someone hurt?" He didn't even bother to tell the person, a pretty blonde from the Bluebell school, that he was leaving, before letting me drag him away.

"This way," I told him, as I pushed a bit of desperation into my voice to make him quicken his pace. "We have to hurry."

"Max," Dale called out to me, his hand tightening in mine. "What's wrong? Did something happen? Please tell me nothing was broken. Headmaster Swordson is going to kill me if I let something happen when he put me in charge."

I shook my head and pulled him harder. "You just have to come to see. I can't explain it."

"Ugh, that doesn't sound good," Dale groaned, but let me drag him through the mob of people.

When we reached where I'd left the guys, it was my feet that faltered. Beth Ann and her minions were pawing all over them, giggling and tossing their hair. They'd traded out their matching dresses from earlier to ones far shorter, but not any more revealing than before. Classy, even when trying to steal someone else's man.

"Come now, Ian," Beth Ann purred, her fingertips trailing up and down his chest. "Just for old times' sake. I remember how we used to have all kinds of fun together."

Ian grabbed Beth Ann's hand and pushed it away, the look in his eyes no longer polite. "I said no. I'm with someone else now."

Beth Ann scoffed, "You mean that half-breed nobody? You can't tell me a trashy girl like that could ever satisfy you."

My teeth gritted together, and I was about to lay into the redheaded witch when Paul stepped in. He moved in close to his brother, using both of their forms to look down at her. "My brother said no. Don't you have a fiancé to be entertaining? I don't think your parents would be too happy to know you were causing a scene."

"Mind your own business, Paul Broomstein. You're just jealous that I always found your brother more appealing than you." Beth Ann sniffed and poked a finger at Paul.

Paul barked a laugh. "Measles are more attractive than you, Beth Ann. Besides, we're taken. All three of us." Paul's eyes flicked over Beth Ann's head to me, a happy grin on his face. "And here she comes now."

Beth Ann slowly turned to where I stood with Dale, her eyes widening slightly before they narrowed. "Her? Y'all can't all be dating her."

"We can and we are," Ian answered, as he moved away from Beth Ann to put an arm around my waist before he kissed my cheek. "Max is plenty enough for all of us, so you can stop trying to harass me. I won't budge."

A gleeful warmth filled me at his words, and I tried not to look smugly at Beth Ann.

Her face contorted with anger as her pale skin started to turn a molten purple. When all four guys were around me, she huffed.

"Fine. Your loss." Beth Ann flicked her hair over her shoulder. "Ladies!" she called to her minions, before turning on her heel and disappearing into the crowd.

I waved at her back, unable to help the smirk on my lips before grabbing a hold of Ian. As I pushed up on my tiptoes, I pressed my lips to his cheek and grinned. "I love you."

Ian stared at me for a second, and then I realized what I said. My face heated and I ducked my eyes down, licking my lips as I tried to keep from panicking.

"I mean, uh... you know... uh..."

"Max," Ian said my name with a softness I'd never heard before, as he tipped my chin up so I met his eyes. "I love you too."

My chest swelled with emotion, and for a moment, I forgot about everyone else around us. I jumped into his arms, my arms wrapping around his neck as I pulled him close. My tongue attacked Ian's mouth, as he gripped my hips and kissed me back with equal fervor.

It didn't last long before Dale interrupted by clearing his throat and poking me on the shoulder. I reluctantly pulled away from Ian, my lips swollen and sensitive from our kissing.

"Yeah?" My voice was husky and breathy, my body already wanting to move things a step further.

Dale frowned at me, his brow furrowed. "Didn't you have an emergency?"

The tone of his voice surprised me. It was sharper than usual. Almost as if he were upset. Was Dale… jealous? It was the first time I'd told any of them that I loved them, so I wouldn't be surprised if he was. It wasn't like it was planned though. It'd just come out. Still…

"Uh, yeah…" I shifted out of Ian's arm and gave him a guilty smile. "I lied. I was… well, we," I gestured to the others with a bashful shrug of my shoulders, "were kidnapping you."

Instead of being happy like I thought he would be, Dale's lips twisted down further. His eyes narrowed and his nostrils flared as his hands tightened into fists by his sides.

"You were kidnapping me?" He cocked his head to the side, his words coming out slowly as if he couldn't comprehend what I said.

"Yes…?" I drawled out, unsure of where this was going.

"So, you pulled me away from my post, one that the Headmaster himself gave me, because why? You wanted to?" Dale snapped, making me wince. I opened my mouth to defend myself, but he cut me off. "No, you may think the world revolves around you because Merlin knows we've been making you feel that way, but some of us aren't in this school on our parents' money."

He thumbed at his own chest. "I have responsibilities. I'm on a scholarship, in case you forgot. I can't just screw off because I have an itch I need to have scratched."

"Hey, now—" Paul tried to defend me, but Dale just turned his angry gaze on him.

"Stay out of it, Broomstein. You're just as bad as Max. You elites have it so easy. Don't want to go to class? Pfft. Teachers look the other way." Dale's voice grew louder, and we began to draw a crowd. "Cause a small fire on campus? Who cares? Your parents will donate to the academy. None of you can say you know what it means to work for something you want so badly and then, when you get it, to be treated like crap for trying to keep it."

I stepped forward and reached my hand out to touch him. "Dale, I never said that." My eyes moved to the onlookers, and I laced my fingers with Dale's. "Let's go somewhere else and talk. I'm really sorry. I didn't mean to make you feel like your job wasn't important."

Dale's hard eyes softened slightly, and his fingers tightened around mine as he jerked his head with a nod. "I know. I... I'm just so tired of it all."

I smoothed my hand down his arm and hugged his side to my chest. "I know."

"Come on." Ian gestured his head toward the exit. "I think we all need to unwind a bit."

After giving the quad a cursory glance, Dale let out a hard breath, more of a sigh really, before following Ian. Aidan and Paul brought up the rear as we moved through the crowd. Most of them turned away from us, more interested in partying than some melodrama going on. The only ones who seemed particularly interested were Sabrina, with an amused smirk on her lips, and Beth Ann who watched with hawk-like intensity.

I refused to think about what that could mean and focused more on Dale. He needed reassurance, and I was just the woman to do it.

Ian led the way as we made our way through the quad and out to the hallway. I wasn't sure where he thought we were going, but I trusted Ian knew what he was doing. None of the others tried to squeeze in on my other side or tried to pull my attention from Dale. They seemed to understand that Dale needed me more right now and were okay with it.

I appreciated that. I hated to think that there would be animosity between the guys. I'd always thought that we'd stay together until it didn't work anymore. I liked to think that day would never come, but sometimes you can't predict what the loves in your life will do.

When we turned down another hallway, I realized where we were heading—Ian's room. It was as good of a place as any to hang out in. Ian did have a sitting room, something that I certainly didn't have, and part of me wondered if it was just because of who he was or because of his level in the school.

"Welcome to my humble abode!" Ian smirked as he pushed open the door to his room and swept an arm inside. The dark blue couches were the same as before, but this time, someone had filled the coffee table and desk with drinks and snacks. Almost as if they knew we would be coming back here.

I asked Ian as much.

As he glanced in my direction, Ian lifted a shoulder. "I might have used a little spell to make sure we had everything we needed tonight..."

"Everything, huh?" Paul lifted one of the potions sitting off to the side with a few charms on cords.

"Are those...?" I arched a brow.

"Yep," Ian said with a pop at the end. "No little wizards or witches until after graduation."

I rolled my eyes. "You're a bit presumptuous, aren't you?"

Ian winked as he shoved his hands into his pockets. "Hey, I always hope for the best, and it's always better to be prepared than… well, you know." He moved his hands in front of him, blowing his cheeks out as he held his hands out like he was holding a big ball.

I shook my head and laughed at that. After I got that out of me, I turned to Dale. "Want something to drink?" I released his arm and moved over to the table of refreshments. "It looks like Ian went all out over here." I shot the wizard in question an appreciative smile.

Ian winked at me again before turning back to Aidan where they were discussing something to do with the games. New rules or something. Dale followed me, his eyes perusing the drinks available. His hand wrapped around a bottle of purple liquid with a label that had a picture of a cartoon man, his eyes heavy-lidded and a lazy grin on his lips.

I picked a pink one, and when I took a sip, it tasted like I had an actual piece of bubble gum in my mouth. A fullness filled my chest, and I put a hand on my heart seconds before a large belch came out. The burp turned into a bubble, pink and shiny as it floated away. My eyes moved to the bottle in my hand, and I rolled my eyes.

"Figures, I'd get one of the ones with side effects like bubble burbs." I showed Dale the picture on the side of the character surrounded by pink bubbles.

"You have to be careful with those things," Paul warned me from the couch, his hand already holding a dark brown colored bottle. "If you drink too many, you'll end up floating yourself to the ceiling."

My nose wrinkled at the thought before I took another tentative sip. I belched again and sighed dramatically before putting the bottle back down. "I think I'll just stick with water since I have bad luck with these things."

But when I glanced back at the table, I didn't see any water in the mixture of rainbow-colored drinks. Of course not. I sighed once more before closing my eyes and pushing my magic up and out. I held my hand out like I was holding a cup, and a moment later, a bottle of water I had in my bedroom teleported into my hands.

"You're getting better at that." Dale nodded toward my hand. "Most don't master conjuring the smallest of objects, let alone from the other side of the school."

I lifted a shoulder, a smile playing on my lips as I took a drink of my water. When I swallowed, I walked across the room and sat next to Paul. I threw my legs over his lap and leaned against the side of the couch.

"So, what are we going to do now?"

Paul stroked his hand up and down my leg, teasing beneath my skirt as his fingertips trailed along my inner thigh. "Whatever you want to do, Max. This is your party."

I threw my head back and laughed before I leaned my arm on the back of the couch while taking another drink of my water. All four pairs of eyes were on me now, and if they had been wolves, I'd say they were circling me, watching to see what my next move would be.

I should have been nervous to have all four of them together at once like this. It was uncharted territory for me and way out of my comfort zone. One on one I was great at. Two on one, I was getting used to. However, four on one? I didn't even know how to make it work, let alone figure out how I felt about it. I mean, we were bound to get to this point, weren't we?

"Max," Ian's voice called out, and my eyes drifted to him. "Stop overthinking it."

"I'm not—"

"Yes, you are." Paul's hand tightened on my thigh, jerking my attention back to him. "We all want you. Don't you want us?"

I swallowed thickly, licked my lips, and nodded.

Paul shrugged a shoulder. "Then that's all we need to know, right?" He stopped looking at me long enough to get signs of confirmation from the others. When Paul's eyes landed back on mine, they were darker, as if he knew what was coming before it even happened. I wasn't even sure what that was. All I knew was that I wanted them.

Maybe Paul was right. Maybe that was all that mattered.

Dale was the first one to move. He pulled his glasses from his face and sat them on the refreshment table before his hands went to his shirt. As he stepped forward, he unbuttoned each button in time with his steps. Finally, he stopped before me on the couch, reached out, and took the bottle of water from my hand. After setting it on the coffee table, Dale took my now empty hand and placed it on his firm abs, urging me to touch and caress him.

I chewed on my lower lip as I moved my fingers along the warmth of his skin, enjoying the way Dale sucked in a breath whenever I moved too close to his pants. I could see the outline of his erection beneath his pants, and suddenly, I wanted him naked before me.

I glanced over at Ian and Aidan. They had stopped talking and were just watching me... watching me touch Dale. Both had matching looks of arousal and desire on their faces as they watched me move my hands to Dale's pants. Confidence surged through me as I unsnapped his pants and drew down the zipper, the sound of it the only thing in the room besides our breathing.

When I reached inside of Dale's pants and released his cock, Dale moaned. I matched that sound as Paul slid his fingers a bit higher to find the crease of my legs and my soaked panties. Slowly, my hand moved up and down Dale's length, and Paul's fingers moved in time with mine. Dale's and my breathing picked up, and my thighs spread farther of their own accord. My eyes never left Dale's face, even as my head fell back against the couch's arm. His gaze switched between watching me pleasure him and watching Paul rub my panties, now visible between my spread legs.

A shadow fell over me and I reluctantly pulled my gaze from Dale to its source—Aidan standing above me. He leaned down until he was almost kneeling, and his mouth met mine in an unhurried kiss. I reached up with my free hand, putting it around his neck to pull him closer as our tongues slid against one another.

It was only a few moments into our kiss when something warm and wet pressed itself to my clit. I gasped and pulled away from Aidan long enough to see Ian's head between my legs. Paul held my panties to the side with one hand and the other probed at my entrance, my insides clenching around the searching digit. I gasped again as Ian sucked harder on me, and my hand on Dale faltered but didn't stop. Aidan captured my next moan with another kiss, pulling my attention to him once more.

It was an odd thing, trying to kiss Aidan while my hand moved over Dale's cock, all while a raging inferno of pleasure flared to life between my thighs. I was surprised that I was able to multitask so well. I'd never been one to be able to split my attention before, but I'd had plenty of practice lately dating all four of the wizards around me. It made me more assured that I could do this.

My orgasm ripped through me and I had to release Aidan's mouth to let out a scream that I was sure could be heard down in the quad. It certainly made the room shake and the lights flicker around us. I still haven't gotten a hold on my magic enough to keep it together when I was, well, falling apart.

However, it didn't seem to faze my wizards, all of them too intent on making me come apart. Dale came shortly after, spurting his release on my hand. Before I had a chance to worry about it, Dale spelled it away, as if it had never happened.

"That's handy," I pointed out with a small lazy smile.

Dale leaned down and kissed my mouth as he cupped one of my breasts in his palm. "Magic does come in handy occasionally. Get it? Handy?" He grinned like he was the first person ever to make a sex joke.

I laughed anyway.

After that, Dale moved over to an empty armchair and flopped down, leaving his shirt and pants undone even as he put his cock away. The other three moved as if they had planned it beforehand. Aidan lifted me up off the couch for a second before sitting me back down... but this time, I was straddling Paul. My hot center cried out with pleasure as it settled against Paul's exposed length. He must have magicked his clothes off in the brief second I'd been in the air.

Behind me, I sensed movement seconds before I felt it. Ian climbed on to the couch, his bare chest pressed to my back. I glanced over my shoulder at him with the sheer desire to see his naked, muscular chest. His hands moved over my hips, pushing my dress up and over my head before I had a say in the matter. My strapless bra was next to go, popped open and discarded without a thought. Aidan's hands replaced my bra, once more being the one in charge of cupping and rolling my nipples between his fingers. Not that he seemed to mind, the tent in his pants showed just how much he enjoyed his assigned position.

Ian's fingers went for my panties, but Dale stopped him.

"Wait." He twisted his wrist and then the next thing I knew, my panties were off my body and in his hand. Dale rubbed them between his fingers before shoving them into his pockets. "Proceed."

"Weirdo." Ian rolled his eyes but didn't stop what he was doing. His mouth moved over my neck and shoulders, making me angle my head to the side. Another set of hands took my hips and lowered me down until the head of Paul's cock teased my entrance. I let out a little breathy gasp as Paul entered me, stretching me until I was full and needy for him.

"Lovely," Ian whispered against my neck, and I turned my ear to him. "Have you ever...?" His voice trailed off as his fingers slid along my ass crack.

I shook my head, my hips bucking as I needed to move. Paul's fingers tightened on my hips, and he felt the ache with me.

At my answer, Ian removed his hand for a second, and then a moment later they returned, but this time with a cool gel. Ian moved the gel between my cheeks and circled around the tight ring back there. First, one digit slipped inside, and as he moved it around, the sensation made me rock against Paul's length. Both of us groaned at the movement, my hands tightening on the end of the couch arm as I leaned forward to give Ian more access to my backside. When the second finger joined the first one, a feeling of fullness and a slight burning made me whimper. Ian kissed my shoulder, smoothing a hand down my back as he moved inside of me.

"Almost there, Max. Just one more. I promise, you're going to like this." Ian placed open-mouthed kisses on my shoulder and neck, one hand sneaking around to stroke between my legs as he added the third and final digit.

"Ah!" My eyes squeezed shut and I pushed back against Ian's hand at the same time as my hips jolted forward. My body was at war with itself. One part wanted the fullness and the other part begged for relief. That's when the sound of a zipper lowering made my eyes open.

Aidan had his length in his hand, stroking it up and down as his eyes focused intently on me. I licked my lips, my eyes flickering between his face and cock. My body wasn't so concerned about the fullness now as I quickly became used to it, and my hips shifted along, which caused Paul to groan.

As I reached for Aidan and my mouth parted to take him in, Ian replaced his fingers with the head of his length. That's when Aidan and Ian pushed into me at the same time, one filling my mouth while the other one filled places no one had ever been before.

For a second, my eyes jumped over to Dale. The wizard had his glasses back on his face as he watched us, his hand wrapped around his cock and moving it in time to our movements. Then we were a tangled, pulsing organism, moving and thrusting as one. Flesh smacked against flesh. Sweat dripped between us, making everything slicker and hotter.

I couldn't tell where I started, and they began. I just knew that I was a second away from bursting into a million pieces, and I didn't care if I ever got put back together again.

Chapter 11

I WOKE UP IN Ian's bed to a combination of warm heat between my thighs and a pounding from somewhere beyond Ian's bedroom. I quickly learned that the warmth at my core came from Aidan's head buried between my legs, his tongue switching between teasing my clit and circling my entrance.

Gasping, my hand reached for his shoulder, and my fingers dug into the thick muscle there as I bucked my hips. Aidan didn't particularly seem to care about my moving, unlike Dale the control freak, who would have had me pinned down until I came when he wanted me to. No, Aidan was more than happy to reach around and cup my ass, attacking my slit with even more fervor.

My eyes closed tight, and my chest rose and fell rapidly, not bothered at all that the covers had fallen off at some point. Or rather pulled off, most likely by Aidan and his wandering mouth.

Ah. God, yes. Not that I was complaining. No siree. I'd be happy to wake up this way every morning. Fuck!

My toes curled and my body tensed up just before an explosion of pleasure ripped through my form, shaking the bed and everything in Ian's room with it. With a sigh, my eyelashes fluttered open and I gave Aidan an appreciative smile. He moved up from his place on the bed, his length already bare since his pants were still somewhere amongst the discarded clothes on the floor and living area.

As Aidan crawled up the bed over my body, I noticed we weren't the only two in the bedroom. A quick glance to my left showed both Broomstein brothers butt ass naked— Oh, what a sight that was —and passed out next to me on the bed, while Dale was curiously missing.

I didn't have a chance to wonder about that too much as Aidan settled his hips between my thighs. I greedily welcomed him, slanting my mouth over his. As my tongue laved his lips, the head of his cock pushed at my aching heat, but didn't move all the way in.

"Are you sore?" Aidan asked with that extra care he always seemed to have. His large fingers caressed the side of my face, and I leaned into his touch.

I took inventory of my body and realized that besides being a bit sensitive, I didn't hurt. In fact, even though I'd been stretched more than I'd been in my entire sexual experience, I wanted more. And with Aidan being the only one of my wizards I hadn't officially had sex with, I was more than eager to have him inside of me. Now.

As I pushed my hips toward him so he entered me just a bit, I groaned out, "Not a bit."

"Good," Aidan grunted out, before pushing completely inside of me. My legs spread farther to accommodate him, my hands grappling at his wide shoulders as he moved inside of me. The bed shifted with every thrust, and I was surprised the brothers didn't wake up from the force of it or the low keening sound coming from the back of my throat as Aidan reached down between us and pressed his thumb down on my bundle of nerves.

My eyes shifted to the side and locked onto Ian's hazel ones. I licked my lips and kept my eyes on him as Aidan leaned down and latched his mouth onto my nipple, pulling it between his teeth and making me gasp in a mixture of pleasure and pain. My eyes shot back to the pale blue eyes of the man fucking me to see a fierceness there.

"Look at me," Aidan growled. "Let them watch me take you."

I nodded, my mouth falling open as my hips jerked up against his hand and the thickness surging inside of me. Just as my world went spinning out of control, the door to the bedroom burst open, and a collective gasp reached my ears. In the middle of falling apart, I didn't have enough shits to give to see who had interrupted us, but there was a quick apology before the door shut with a resounding slam.

Ian's eyes jerked away from Aidan and me, as he cursed and jumped out of the bed. "Fuck, fuck, fuck. Hairy Merlin balls."

My orgasm quickly cooled at the way Ian was freaking out, so I looked to Aidan for an explanation. Aidan didn't answer, he only lifted a shoulder before shifting off me. I felt a bit bad that our first time together had been marred with whoever had come barging into the room, but I made a promise to make it up with many more times in the future.

"Bro," Paul groaned, still partly asleep, "shut the fuck up."

"Get your ass up," Ian shouted back as he threw Paul's pants at his face. "Our parents just walked into our bedroom where Max was currently getting screwed by my best friend."

Paul's eyes shot open and jumped out of bed, freaking out as his brother had. It would have been funny if it hadn't been such a shit show.

I got out of bed myself and went about putting my own clothes on as I watched them scurrying around the room like a pair of chickens with their heads cut off. "Why are your parents here?"

Ian answered me with a scowl. "How the fuck would I know? They were on another one of their trips. They never show up for our birthdays, let alone a surprise visit. I want to know how they got in here in the first place." Ian shot a glare at the door just as it opened and revealed a red-faced Dale.

"That would be my fault... or rather the Headmaster's." Dale was already dressed but looked rumpled and like... well... he'd spent the night getting drunk and screwing his girlfriend. Which he had.

My body tingled at the reminder and I had to blink my eyes to make the vivid imagery of him and Paul taking me together shortly after Ian and Paul had disappear. As if he knew what I was thinking, Dale's green eyes flicked over to me appreciatively, taking in my mostly nude form. I'd only been able to find my panties so far and the fact that they were in here and not in the living room was a mystery. The rest of my clothes were probably strewn around out there.

"Why didn't you tell them to wait?" Paul snapped. He jerked his shirt over his head and then ran his hands through his hair, but no amount of preening would fix the rooster's butt coming out of his head. He'd need a shower to tame that mess of hair.

"You don't think I didn't try?" Dale crossed his arms over his chest and narrowed his eyes. "I told them you were sleeping. They didn't care. They insisted on seeing you." Dale shrugged helplessly. "Headmaster Swordson was with them, I couldn't say no."

Ian opened his mouth to argue again, but I cut him off as I stepped between the two of them. "There's no use arguing over it now. Just finish getting dressed and we can deal with it then."

Ian and Dale locked eyes over my head, but then Dale nodded and walked back into the living room. While the guys went about finding their own clothing, I followed Dale into the living room for mine. My bra, to my mortification, was by the front door, which meant there was no way the Headmaster or the Broomstein's hadn't seen it on their way to the bedroom. My dress was shoved down inside the couch cushions. When I pulled it out, it was so wrinkled that I wasn't sure that a spell could get it clean and looking like new. Regardless, I had nothing else to wear, and I was too hungover to magic up anything for myself now.

"So, I'm assuming my parents went to the Headmaster's office?" Paul asked, as he walked into the sitting area and found his shoes, shoving each foot inside. "I can't imagine they would hang around the campus anywhere else."

"I don't know." Dale shrugged helplessly. "They didn't say. They were too astounded by what they saw to really get much of anything out."

Ian groaned as he appeared in his bedroom doorway. "Great. Just what I need, another reason for them to give me shit." He sauntered over to Paul and clapped him on the shoulder. "At least this time I'm not the only one in hot water. Welcome to the black sheep side of the family. You'll find it's cold and, well, a lot more fun." He chuckled as his brother made a face and pushed Ian's hand off him.

"Come on, let's get this over with." Paul adjusted the buttons on his shirt before sighing and walking to the door. "Are you going to wait here?"

I cocked my head to the side, thinking. "No. I don't think so. I need to shower and then I'll probably go to the library and start on that paper for Pottery class." When Paul raised a brow, I laughed. "I know, I know, but it's due Monday and I don't want to fail. Text me about what happens, okay?"

Paul nodded before leaving the room, and Ian winked at me before disappearing behind him. Aidan approached me and offered me his hand. I blinked up at him with a slow smile before sliding my palm into his larger one. "Walk me to my room?"

He nodded and directed us to the door.

I held a hand out to Dale as we passed by him, but Dale shook his head. "I should head to the office too. Try and see if anything happened last night that I missed during our..." He trailed off and his face turned red.

I bit my lip to keep from laughing at how cute he was. The last thing he needed was me making fun of him, especially with how serious he was about his job. Still, I couldn't get over the urge to kiss his face, so did. That only made his lips curve out into a broad grin as he shoved his glasses up his nose.

"Have lunch with me?" I arched a brow at him, Aidan waiting by my side until I was ready to go.

Dale shoved his hands in his pockets, his shoulders bunching up as he nodded. "Sure, if I can get away. I'll let you know."

"'Kay."

With that, I let Aidan lead me from the room and down the hallway. A glance at my phone told me it was already well past breakfast. We'd slept way longer than we should have, but then again, we had drunk a lot of alcohol last night and the energy we expelled from all our activities... I flushed hotly in remembrance.

Most of the students looked about as good as us—pale and barely holding their breakfast in. Some weren't even pretending they weren't hungover, their heads buried in their hands or sleeping in their chairs in the quad, hoodies pulled over their heads. Aidan's arm was hot and heavy against my lower back, and even though we had just had sex, I wanted him to touch me even more.

"Max."

My eyes jerked up to Aidan's pale blue ones. They were darker than usual, and his tongue darted out to lick his lips as if he could read the thoughts going through my mind. My face grew hotter the longer he stared into my eyes, and I almost forgot that we were in the quad, surrounded by all the other hungover students.

Aidan paused and turned to me, his large hand reaching out to cup my face. His thumb stroked along my bottom lip, and unintentionally, I licked my lips at the same time, touching the skin of his thumb. Aidan sucked in a breath, and for a second, I thought he would kiss me, or better yet push me into the nearest classroom and have an encore of what we did this morning. Then a few of the Cali wizards burst out laughing as a red fog spewed out of one of the guy's can of soda. Coughing students scattered, and the moment between Aidan and me was broken.

With a sigh, Aidan clasped his hand with mine. "Let's go."

We made it back to my room in record time, but before I could open the door, Trina swung it open with a weird grin and glazed over eyes. "Max, babe! You've got to get in here and try these brownies. They are the best thing since magic vibrators!"

I arched a brow at her and then looked to Aidan. "There are magic vibrators?"

Chapter 12

BEFORE AIDAN COULD ANSWER my question, Trina yanked me into our dorm room. I gave Aidan a worried look over my shoulder as he followed me in and shut the door behind us.

Trina giggled and she released my hand, skipping away to pick up a white plate with blue flowers on the edges. On the plate were some rather innocent looking brownies. They smelled delicious, but there were only a few left.

"See?" Trina offered me the plate with a cheesy grin. "Don't they look scrumptiliumptious?" She picked one up and took a bite, moaning as she moved it around in her mouth. "They're so goooood." The way she moaned and wiggled in place made me think of sex and not in a good way.

After giving Aidan a 'what the fuck' look, I shifted in place and forced a smile. "Uh, yeah, Trina, they look good. Where did you get them?" I took the plate from her and handed it to Aidan, thankful that Trina was so absorbed with her current piece to let me.

I had a feeling if she wasn't, then she'd bite my damn hand off for taking it away.

"Oh!" Trina's eyes got large, waving a hand at me. "At the party last night," she gave me a sly grin and winked, "which you missed most of, you dirty, dirty girl." After she took another bite, Trina licked her fingertips and crossed one leg over the other, not even bothered by the fact that she was now floating midair.

"Uh, is that supposed to happen?" I asked Aidan, becoming increasingly more worried by the second.

Aidan sniffed the plate, and his nose wrinkled up before looking over at Trina who had continued to chitchat about the party. "Brownie Madness."

"Huh?" I arched a brow and pulled my lower lip into my mouth, chewing on it. "Is that bad?"

"Not bad!" Trina giggled and fell back in the air, rolling from side to side. "It's great!"

I ignored her and turned back to Aidan. "Should I be worried? She's not going to be stuck like this forever, will she?"

"No." Aidan shook his head and handed me the plate back. "It'll wear off."

I took the plate and tilted my head to the side, wondering what exactly they were. They couldn't be too bad if Trina had them, right? She wouldn't purposely eat something bad for her. My eyes snapped back to my roommate, and I waved my hands in her face.

"Trina. Trina." I snapped my fingers until she stopped laughing long enough to look at me. "Where did you get the brownies?"

"I already told you, silly. The party." Trina snorted and rubbed her nose, which kept wiggling afterward until it almost jumped off her face.

I sighed impatiently and grabbed her nose to make it stop. "I know at the party, but where?"

Trina shrugged. "On the refreshment table." Then a slow smile curved up her face. "Someone set them out and just left them there. I was lucky I saw them when I did before the Cali's got a hold of them. They're hot for this stuff."

"Cali's?" My brows shot up my forehead and then a thought came to me. Twisting around so fast that my head spun, I gaped at Aidan. "Are these like magical pot brownies?"

Trina snorted and laughed like a donkey... a bit too convincingly.

I spun back the other way, the contents of my stomach rolled around, and I had to pause to breathe in and out a few times before my eyeballs finally adjusted in my head to see Trina with the face of a donkey. She still had her braided black hair at least, but that multitude of braids fell around her snout like a donkey's ears. At least her body was still unchanged.

"A-Aidan," I stuttered, my hands tightening on the plate, "is that supposed to happen?"

Aidan let out a huff. "It can. Brownie Madness has the same kind of properties as human marijuana, but with a few extra magical add-ons. One of those is," he clucked his tongue and gestured to Trina, "random morphing."

"Will she turn back?" I squealed as I blinked at Trina. The moment I asked the question, Trina's face morphed back to normal. Well, kind of. Her eyes had now turned bright pink. "Trina, how many of these brownies did you eat?"

Trina lifted her hand up and started to count on her fingers. "One, two, fifty-two million. I don't know. Numbers don't matter. The only thing that matters are these yummy, yummy brownies." Trina's hand reached out to try to grab the plate from me, but I pulled them back as I stepped into Aidan's embrace.

"No, I think you've had enough." Just seconds before she came for me, Aris tinged a warning. I dodged her grabbing hands one way and then the other, but she kept coming. It was only when Aidan took the plate from my hands and held it high in the air that she left me alone.

Unfortunately, with her new ability to float, even Aidan's height wasn't enough to dissuade her. Trina flew over my head, making me duck down to avoid her kicking feet, and tried for the plate once more. Aidan held the plate with one hand and held Trina back with the other, his large palm covering her face.

"Let me go!" Trina's muffled voice cried out as her hands jerked around trying to find the plate. "I want them. They're mine."

I tugged on her leg and growled. "Knock it off. You're making a fool of yourself over brownies. Besides, aren't you trying to lose weight? Libby won't like you if you get a bigger butt than hers."

Bringing up Trina's girlfriend at least got a reaction out of her. She pulled away from Aidan's grasp, and her hands dropped to her butt. Her mouth widened as she palmed it.

"What? No? It's not big. It's fine. Right?" She floated back down to the ground, and her panicked eyes searched mine. "Tell me, Max. You have to keep those brownies away from me. I can't lose Libby. I just can't!"

Her eyes watered and I drew her in for a hug, waving Aidan away with the plate. We needed to get the brownies as far away from Trina as possible before she flipped her switch on us again. Aidan took the plate over to the trash can as I patted Trina on the back.

"There, there," I soothed. "You're fine. Libby will still like you. I promise."

Aidan dumped the brownies into the trash and snapped his fingers. The contents of the trash can caught on fire, and the flash of the flames drew Trina's attention. Aris went crazy as it tried to warn me of the fire that we had created. The stupid idiot.

"What are you doing? You can't light a fire in here." Trina scowled and then her eyes widened. "Wait, are those my brownies? You can't burn them. They're all I have!"

Trina tried to run toward the trash can. I looped my arms around her waist and pulled her back to me to keep her from trying to shove her hands into the flames. If she wanted those brownies bad enough to burn herself, then they couldn't have been as harmless as I thought.

Aidan waved his hand over the trash can once more, and the fire went out.

That's when Trina kicked me in the shins, something my guardian light did not warn me of, and I was forced to let her go. Trina dived for the trash can and grabbed a handful of what were now charcoal blocks.

As she brushed them off, she cried out, "They're still good. See? They're okay. Just a bit burnt." Trina took a bite of one and forced a smile. "See? Ugh... they're... they're horrible. Fuck. Yuck." She spat out the burnt brownie into the trash and wiped her tongue so aggressively, I thought she might rip her own tongue out.

As I chuckled at Trina's ridiculousness, I shook my head and crossed my arms under my chest. "Well, serves you right. Getting high on school property and all."

Trina glared at me and I wrinkled my nose, sticking my tongue out at her. It was Aidan's sudden jolting movement across the room that interrupted our childish staring contest. The plate Aidan still had in his hand looked like it was trying to jerk away from him. And rather aggressively too. He had both hands around the plate now, his teeth gritted as he attempted to keep it from flying off.

"What's going on?" I cocked my head to the side, pushing past Trina to stand by Aidan.

"Return spell," Aidan grunted out.

"A return spell?" I stared at the plate as it tried with all its might to get away from Aidan. "What's that?"

Trina let out an obnoxious giggle. "It's trying to get back to its owner. Let it go! Let it go!" Trina clapped her hands and snorted, just before her nose morphed into a pig's snout. She fingered it with curiously before giggling and snorting once more.

I glanced from my high-on-magic roommate to my boyfriend. I hummed and tapped my chin with my finger. "So, whoever made the brownies must own the plate, right?"

Aidan grunted in response.

"There are bluebonnets on the plate. Obviously they came from them. They're such nice girls. So put together. So posh. Like walking mermaids." Trina sighed, her nose morphing back as her hair faded into a pale pink.

I rolled my eyes. "There are more than a dozen Bluebonnets on campus right now for the games. I want to know which one exactly brought these brownies. None of our students would have had the balls to put drugged goods out at a school party."

Trina cackled as her hair switched again from pink to yellow. "Fuck no. Swordsmen would have our asses. He has a strict no-tolerance policy. Oh no!" Trina's eyes widened, her hands slapping to both cheeks. "I'm going to get suspended! Or worse, expelled!" Trina's hair went back to normal, but her face went red and purple as she panicked. Grabbing my hands, Trina jerked them up and down. "Max, you have to help me! If I get kicked out, my parents are going to kill me! I can't get caught like this. I just can't!" Big fat tears rolled down her face, changing colors as they went.

I patted Trina on the back before pulling her into a hug. "There, there. It'll be fine. I won't let anything happen to you."

"You won't?" Trina sniffed and rubbed her nose on my shoulder, leaving a snotty line of wetness there.

Ew.

Holding back my grimace, I pulled away and nodded solemnly. "I promise. You stay here while Aidan and I find out who sent the brownies." I shot a look of disdain at the plate. "They obviously have it out for someone."

Trina snorted, but this time it was more sarcastic and less manic. "Probably trying to cut down on the competition. They're not known for playing fair."

Aidan grunted his agreement.

"Okay." I inclined my head and led Trina to her bed. While tucking her in, I said, "You just lay here and sleep it off. We'll get to the bottom of this. Don't let anyone in our room, okay?"

Trina sniffed and in a small voice replied, "'Kay."

With a sigh, I turned back to Aidan, about to tell him to let go of the plate, but then I stopped. "Hold on. I've gotta change or I'm going to lose my mind." Without the time or privacy to switch clothes the normal way, I pulled on that ball of light inside of me and pushed it out, focusing on the clothes I was wearing. The dress from last night warmed against my skin before it lengthened and encased my legs. The skirt transformed into jeans and the strapless top became a regular, old Winchester Academy t-shirt, fully decked out in blue and white, with the owl Crest on the right-hand pocket.

"There." I sighed as I smoothed my hands down my new clothes. "That's better." I still needed a shower, but clean clothes were definitely a step in the right direction. Turning to Aidan, I pointed at the plate. "Let it—"

"The door," Trina's voice called out, cutting me off.

"Huh?" I looked over my shoulder at her.

Trina jerked her chin toward the other side of the room. "You need to open the door, or the plate won't have anywhere to go."

My eyes followed where she'd gestured, and my eyes widened slightly. "Oh. Right. Good idea." I hurried over to the door and pulled it open before waving a hand to Aidan. "Alright. Let it go."

Aidan released the plate, and it automatically zoomed out of his hands and out the doorway. We had to run after it to make sure it didn't get too far ahead of us. I barely had time to get the door shut behind me before it zipped down the hallway.

"Come on, this way!" I called to Aidan, as I took off after the plate. It was dodging students and bumping into walls without getting a single crack in it. Must be another spell, I thought to myself as I hurried after the flying dish.

We chased it through the elite hallway and into another hallway that was reserved for out-of-town guests. It made sense since the plate belonged to a Bluebonnet, and I had a sneaky suspicion I knew who the plate belonged to.

The plate came to a door and banged against it over and over, almost to the point where I thought it might break. Aidan and I waited near it for the door to open. We didn't have long to wait before the cream-colored door opened to reveal a familiar, smiling redhead.

"Beth Ann," I groaned. "I should have known."

The plate dropped from the air and into Beth Ann's waiting hands. She stared at us with her bright green eyes and a curious look on her face. "Should have known what?"

I took the few steps to her door and snapped, "That you'd be behind those horrible brownies."

"Brownies?" She cocked her head to the side as her lips pursed into a pretty little confused pout. "I can assure y'all that I have no idea what you're talkin' about."

I growled. My fingers curled into fists at my sides. "Cut the innocent crap. You're the owner of that plate, so it's obvious you brought the drugged brownies to the party last night."

Beth Ann's brows lifted, and a slight tick of her lip was the only obvious show of guilt as she purred, "I really have no clue why you are carryin' on in such a manner. Any number of people could have borrowed my plate. I don't exactly keep it under lock and key. It's a plate, not the holy grail."

She sighed and placed the plate somewhere inside her room before stepping into the hallway and closing the door behind her.

"Now, if y'all are done trying to accuse me of somethin', of what I have no inkling of, I have a lunch to get to with the Broomsteins." She paused to smile at me gleefully. "You have met them, haven't you? You are dating both brothers, after all."

I frowned and crossed my arms over my chest. "They've been out of town and busy. I can't expect them to drop everything to meet me."

"Oh, really?" Beth Ann gave a smug smile as she laced her fingers in front of her. "Well, they must have had a dip in their schedules, because when I called them this morning to have them meet me today, they were more than happy to come."

Ouch. I tried to hold back the wince, but based on Beth Ann's triumphant face, I hadn't been very successful.

"Well, as I said, I have plans. So, if y'all'll excuse me." Beth Ann turned and flipped the length of her hair over her shoulder, smacking me in the face in the process before sauntering down the hallway.

I glared after her. How dare she come here and act like she owned the place? To try and move in on my boyfriend in front of me and then go around making lunch dates with his parents! All to make me look bad of course. It made the magic in me burn through my veins and I could feel the crackling at my fingertips.

Aidan's hand on my shoulder reminded me of the big man's presence and I released some of my anger with a sigh. I gave him a weak smile. "Guess I'm not what the Broomsteins consider acceptable for their sons."

Aidan drew me close to his chest, smoothing his hand over my hair without a word.

I liked how Aidan did that. He could calm my nerves and make everything better without having to say anything at all. I could tell just from his embrace that he was here for me, and he didn't agree with Beth Ann or the Broomsteins. Which made me feel slightly better. I needed him in my corner today. Especially if I was going to end up having a run-in with said parents. I could only imagine how that encounter was going to be.

"Come on." I said, and sighed before reluctantly stepping out of Aidan's warm embrace. "I'm starving. I want to find something to eat before I smash something just for the fun of it."

"Trina." Aidan reminded me.

"Oh, yeah, I have to figure out what to do about her too." I thought about it for a few moments. "Think it's like regular pot? You just need time and sleep to wipe it out? Maybe have some food ready for her afterward?"

Aidan grunted.

I took that as a yes.

We headed to the cafeteria hand in hand. Well, more like his large hand engulfed my smaller hand. It didn't bother me, but it did remind me of before and another part of him that was large just like the rest of him. My face heated.

I sneaked a look at Aidan and noticed him watching me. He lifted a brow, which only made me blush even further. This was going to make things even more interesting.

Chapter 13

THE GUEST STUDENTS WEREN'T just there to hang around until the games started, they also took classes with us. That meant I had to see more than my fair share of Beth Ann and her group.

I went to Pottery and there she was. During flying lessons, she was right next to me, bragging about being an All-State champion in Texas. In Advanced Potions, she was at the table behind me. Really, it was getting annoying. I already hated her for her previous attempts to nab Ian when she had a fiancé, but with her always there, constantly bragging, it made things even worse.

I never did get to meet Ian and Paul's parents. They were here for lunch then gone by the next hour. I had to listen to Beth Ann's smug recounting of the lunch every time I came within hearing distance of her—which unfortunately was often.

"Mrs. Broomstein, or Willow as she likes me to call her, is simply a doll," Beth Ann cooed while we sat in the Pottery class a few weeks later. "Willow told me that any time I wanted to meet up to just to let her know. I'd always been her favorite of Ian's girlfriends." Beth Ann gave me a sidelong glance as she said that.

"Max," Dale whispered next to me, touching me on the arm.

"What?" I growled, still glaring daggers at Beth Ann. If I thought I could get away with it, I would curse the bitch to lose all those gorgeous red locks. Then we'd see who the favorite was.

Dale cleared his throat. "Max, stop."

"Huh?" I glanced away from Beth Ann to Dale's amused expression.

He inclined his head toward my hands. "You're kind of killing your pot."

I frowned in confusion as my eyes drifted down. He was right. The pot I'd been trying to create looked more like a big glob of goop from where my fingers had dug into the clay.

I lifted my hands with a sheepish, "Oh. Oops."

Dale smiled at me. "That's okay. I have those days too. Want to talk about it?" He jerked his head toward Beth Ann. Apparently, I hadn't been subtle with my hatred of the redhead.

I sighed dejectedly and shook my head. "Not really. She just drives me nuts."

"I can tell." Dale chuckled as his hands smoothed out the sides of his pot one final time before he slowed the spin of the wheel, bringing it to a stop. "Here. Let me see if we can fix yours."

He leaned over into my area, moving his hands up and down my pot as I moved the wheel with my foot. They had electric ones and even magical pottery wheels, but Pottington claimed it was the lazy way and that we couldn't make a half-decent magical item if we took shortcuts. Things like this needed patience and a deft hand, something I was obviously lacking.

Shooting a look toward our instructor, I hoped she would stay far away from me and my disaster of a pot today. The last thing I needed was another lecture about control, especially not in front of Beth Ann and her minions. I didn't need her to know how much she was affecting me. Ian was mine, and she could schmooze his parents all she wanted, but it wasn't going to change the fact. That was why I resolved right then not to let it bother me anymore.

"And then, Tylus, I mean Mr. Broomstein, invited me to spend Christmas with them up at their house in the Alps! Can you imagine? Being snowed in with nothing but our body heat to keep us warm... I mean, what else could a witch ask for?" Beth Ann flipped her hair, and her friends giggled around her.

"You're so bad," one of the other Bluebonnets cooed and laughed.

Beth Ann smiled and sighed. "I know. It's so easy to get caught up with how magical my life has been, but it's the little things that really matter. You have to know when to let go and when to hold on tight."

"But what about Chad?" a brunette female student asked, making Beth Ann's smile dip.

"What about him?" Beth Ann scoffed. "He'll be there, just as my parents want, but that doesn't mean I shouldn't get to be happy too, right?"

"Right," the Bluebonnets chimed in around her, before each of them focused back on their perfect pots beneath their perfect hands.

"Maxine Mancaster!" Pottington cried out as she rushed to my station. Her eyes widened behind her large glasses, and her hair seemed even wilder and out of control than before. "What have you done to your pot?"

I winced as my eyes went down to the monstrosity I'd created. Not even Dale's help had saved it from my latest bout of rage. Inwardly, I lamented. Maybe I just wasn't meant to make magical items like pots and the like. I should stick with what I know, which sadly wasn't pottery.

"Sorry." I held my hands out on either side of my pot. "It seems to have gotten away from me."

Beth Ann and her group giggled in my direction and I fought back a glower.

Pottington sighed, adjusting her large glasses on her nose. "It's far more than that. You will never be proficient in the magical world if you can't control yourself more than this. It's a delicate task. One that requires patience, respect, and..."

"Practice," the class and I recited by memory. It wasn't the first time she'd lectured us on the three parts of creating. They were something she pounded into our heads the first week we were here and in every single class afterward.

Pottington pursed her lips, her brows furrowing in annoyance. "Yes, and if you, Miss Mancaster, spent a little bit more time focusing on your craft and less on flirting with Mister Varnes," her eyes shot to Dale, who flushed and shifted in his seat, "then you could not only master this task, but all those afterward. I expect better." Her eyes narrowed over her glasses as she waited for me to answer.

I nodded and murmured, "Yes, Professor Pottington. I'll do better in the future."

"See that you do." She spun around and moved on to the next student, clicking her tongue as she criticized their work.

A psst sound drew my eyes from my ruined project to Beth Ann's grinning face.

"What?" I grumbled as I jabbed my fingers into the clay on my wheel top. It didn't matter anymore, class was almost over and the pot wasn't worth saving.

Beth Ann giggled and glanced over her shoulder at her friends before looking back to me. "You really should just drop out. You're too far behind to be anything but mediocre."

"I'm not dropping pottery because of one day," I snapped back with a growl. I could feel my magic swirling in my stomach, and I pushed it down before I got myself in even more trouble.

Beth Ann shook her head and grinned further. "Not this class. The school. Take it from a friend when I tell you, you're not doing yourself or anyone else here any favors by staying. You'd be better off at a human college, then perhaps you could do somethin' worth meanin'." She smirked and eyed my clump of clay. "Though you are providing a public service with your attempts. Who am I to take away from others who might need you to encourage them to do better?"

My teeth grit together, the urge to throw clay at her perfect face was so strong but I shoved it down. Instead, a sickly-sweet smile curled up my lips. "You're right. I am giving a public service, and here's my service to you. You might have a better chance of having a happy marriage if you spen less time trying to kiss ass to your ex-boyfriend's parents, and spent more time with your actual fiancé." I gave a shrug and pouted. "Just saying."

Beth Ann's eyes narrowed and her lips curled into a thin line. Then, while Pottington wasn't looking, a glob of clay magically came hurtling toward me. Thinking quick on my feet, I shoved my magic out as a barrier sending the clay bouncing back off and splattering Beth Ann's hair.

Suddenly, the room burst into laughter. My own mouth spread into a grin as Beth Ann shrieked and jumped up from her chair, her hands trying to grab at the clay in her red hair. Professor Pottington rushed to her side and tried to calm her down. Beth Ann didn't immediately point a finger at me because then she would have to explain why she was throwing clay at me in the first place.

Pottington tried to make the class calm down, but they were too hyped up so she gave up. "Class is dismissed, and next class, I expect you to act like the responsible young adults you are."

Dale stood and held a hand out to me. "Come on, Max."

Still grinning at Beth Ann, I slid my hand into his and did a little hair flip of my own. "Thanks for the advice, Beth Ann."

My words only made Beth Ann freak out even more as Dale ushered me out of the room. When we were safely in the hallway, Dale stopped in the middle of the hall. Bent at the waist, his hands on his knees, his body shook violently.

"Dale?" I tilted my head to the side and reached for him. "Are you okay?"

"Yes," Dale choked out and glanced up, with tears of laughter falling down his face. He removed his glasses and swiped his hand over his eyes. "I'm fine. Oh, Merlin! Max, I could kiss you right now."

I grinned from ear to ear and swayed from side to side. "I wouldn't object to that."

Dale mimicked my expression and wrapped his arms around my waist. "As tempted as I am, I think we better put some distance between us and Beth Ann for now."

I pouted. "But I want a kiss."

Shaking his head, Dale took my hand and drew me down the hallway. "Not usually. But you, my little minx, just attacked a Scarlette and they have bad tempers. I'd blame the red hair but..." He trailed off, running a hand through his own reddish head. "Just hope that Beth Ann doesn't complain to her parents. Believe me, no one wants those soul-sucking medusas here."

My head jerked to him. "You've met them?"

Dale lifted a shoulder, tucking his hands into his pockets as we walked.

"Unfortunately. Since I work for the Headmaster, there are a lot of meetings that involve other schools, and the Scarlettes are big contributors." He snorted and shook his head. "Which is a fancy way of saying they use their money to make sure the schools are teaching what they want. You know, political bullshit."

I hummed and then changed the subject. "So, we have a free period..." I trailed off, giving Dale a coy grin.

Dale held back a grin in return. "Oh, whatever shall we do?"

I opened my mouth to answer back, but almost walked straight into a hard body. "Whoa!" I jumped back into Dale's arms and prepared to glare at the asshole who wasn't paying any mind to where they were going. "Watch it, why don't... Ian?"

The asshole who'd walked right into me was none other than one of my boyfriends. Ian's head slowly turned in my direction, his usually playful eyes tired and his charming mouth turned down in a painful grimace. He didn't seem like himself. His clothes were wrinkled, and he hadn't put anything in his hair, so it looked greasy and unkempt.

Ian blinked several times as if he couldn't focus completely before his lips moved slowly into a halfhearted grin. "Max. There you are."

"Uh, yeah." I gave Dale a sideways glance before moving closer to Ian. "What's going on? I haven't seen you since your parents came to visit. Are you okay?"

Ian grinned lazily, his hand brushing through his hair. "Oh, yeah. I'm fine. Just busy with work. Where have you been?"

Still not completely convinced but not wanting to push, I told him about what happened in pottery class. Ian's brows furrowed, and his hands grabbed my shoulders.

"Don't mess with Beth Ann, Max. I'm serious. She can make life difficult for you. Worse than Sabrina."

My brows furrowed at Ian's warning. "I can handle myself. I'm not going to let some snotty Bluebonnet paw my boyfriend and get away with it."

"Let it go."

The sharp tone of Ian's voice made me pause. "Do you want to be with her?"

Ian's head fell back, and he let out a tired laugh. "No, not at all, but I know how she and her family is, and I'm telling you, it's not worth it. She'll be gone after the games, then everything will go back to normal." He rubbed his hands up and down my arms. "Just leave it alone. For me?"

"How can you ask her to do something like that?" Dale asked with a growl, getting in Ian's face. "She doesn't get to push Max around just because her family has money. None of you do. Max has a right to stand up for herself and for you to tell her not to is... just fucked up, man. How can you even call her your girlfriend?"

Ian looked like he was about to fire back at Dale, but then he grasped his head and closed his eyes, hissing, "Whatever, I... I have to get back to work."

Then before either of us could stop him, Ian was gone.

I gave Dale a worried frown and held his hand tightly. "Well, that was weird."

Chapter 14

MID OCTOBER, I THREW my pen down on the library table and groaned. "This is ridiculous."

"What?" Paul looked away from the papers he was grading, his pen poised in the air.

My eyes narrowed as the source of my irritation filled the air with her nasal voice and ridiculous giggle—Beth Ann. She sat at the table Sabrina and her friends used to sit at, holding court over a few of her friends and more than a handful of guys, some out-of-staters and some from our very own school. They were all holding on to every word Beth Ann said as she entertained them with some inane story or another. Probably talking about the latest sweet tea she and her annoying friends drank.

"So, what's the point of them being here before the games even start?" I jerked my head back around to Paul. Irritation made my face tight as I sighed and threw my hand up. "I mean, all they're doing is hanging around, going to our classes, and... and..."

"Hitting on my brother?" Paul chuckled, a knowing grin on his perfect lips.

I narrowed my gaze on him but didn't answer.

Paul set his pen down and sighed, running his fingers through his hair. "Look, I know you don't like them, but there's not much we can do. They're here until the end of the year whether we like it or not." I opened my mouth to argue, but Paul stopped me. "Believe me, if I could get them gone any faster I would, especially after Beth Ann brought my parents here."

I grimaced. "Yeah. That couldn't have been fun." I chewed on my lower lip and peered down at my book before glancing back up at him, unsure of myself. "About that... your parents hate me, don't they?"

Paul's brows furrowed, and then his mouth opened and closed several times before finally saying, "No, I wouldn't say that. They've never met you, so they don't know you." He reached for my hand and cupped it with his own. Bringing it up to his mouth, Paul pressed a kiss to the top of my knuckles. "Not like I do."

I snorted. "Pfft. Yeah, sure, but they know Beth Ann?"

Paul let out a hard breath before releasing my hands to pick up his pen again. "Beth Ann's family has been involved with ours for a long time, the same way that Sabrina's parents were. You know, if you maybe made more of an effort to mingle with our class, maybe—"

"I'd be a snobby stuck-up witch that wouldn't have attracted you in the first place." I stuck my tongue out at him and winked.

That's when Paul grabbed me around the waist, pulled me into his lap, and kissed me soundly on the mouth. I giggled and curved my fingers along the nape of his neck, leaning into his kiss. Paul's tongue stroked along the edge of my lips and I happily opened up for him, letting out a tiny sound of pleasure. Our mouths tangled with one another and quickly becoming heated. Neither of us seemed to care that we were in public or what we looked like to the others.

Screw them.

Not even Beth Ann could ruin this for me.

The hands on my hips tightened slightly and I could feel Paul's length hardening beneath me. I wiggled against it, causing him to groan and pull me closer. My thighs pressed together as I tried to relieve some of the pressure building there. If we didn't stop soon, we'd end up giving the library a free show, and I didn't feel like getting expelled today.

"Wanna get out of here?" I breathed into Paul's mouth, and rubbed my hardened nipples against his chest. "I still have..." I glanced at my phone. "Thirty minutes before my next class."

Paul groaned and leaned his head back. "I can't. I have to finish these papers and then meet up with Ian. Our parents have been around more often now because of..." He trailed off, his eyes moving over to where Beth Ann sat, but he didn't say her name. Instead, his lips pursed, and his nose crinkled up. "Business."

"Right," I drawled before slipping out of his lap and back into my own seat. Not wanting to argue about Beth Ann, I picked at something else that was bothering me. "How is Ian? I haven't seen him around much. And the few times we've hung out he's seemed really... off."

Humming, Paul stared down at the paper in front of him. There was a sort of seriousness to his expression as a bit of worry tugged at the edges of his lips. It didn't make me feel any better about how Ian had been acting.

The last time we went out, we'd gone to McKee's. Ian had been quiet and looked two seconds away from passing out the whole time. The waitress had to ask him several times what he wanted before he even looked up from his menu to notice her. Forget him listening to anything I said. I felt like I was talking to a brick wall.

"I'm not sure what's going on. He hasn't said anything to me about it." Paul tapped his pen on the top of the table and then released it.

The pen floated in the air and then started to write on the paper for him. I didn't know why he even bothered to do it the normal way if he had magic to do it, but then again, what did I know? Magic was still a new deal for me. For Paul, who had been working magic since he was in diapers, it was just another day in the life. Doing it the human way was probably a novelty for him.

"Well, what about Aidan? Has he said anything?" I stood from the table and gathered my books and notebooks. While Ian hadn't been around much, I'd been spending more time with Aidan and the others. Dale was still busy because of the visitors and all the stupid events the Headmaster thought would bring us closer together with the out-of-staters.

This month's Halloween party came to mind. There was going to be a huge costume party, including a contest to see who had the best costume. Normally, I would have thought nothing of a costume party, let alone a contest, but this was the magical world. I could only imagine how farfetched the students would get with their costumes. Maybe someone would transfigure themselves into an octopus or a mummy? Or maybe they'd invite real live werewolves?

That would be awesome.

"Aidan hasn't said anything either." Paul lifted a shoulder and dropped it. "Besides, it's not like he's much of a talker anyway."

I sighed. "I thought they're supposed to be BFFs? Plus, they're both in the Dark Arts division. Shouldn't Aidan have the four-one-one?" I growled, getting more irritated by the minute. "I don't see Aidan looking like he's having the life sucked out of him." My brows shot up, and my mouth fell open. "Wait, could that be it? Could someone be sucking the life out of Ian? Maybe that group he joined last year?"

Paul shook his head. "Nah, there are strict rules against that kind of stuff. More than likely, he is overworking himself and is just experiencing the normal stress of college life. He is about to graduate, you know?" Paul grabbed the pen and took over marking the papers before him. "I wouldn't worry too much about it."

"I know, but—"

"He's still signed up for the Games, right?" Paul continued to scribble, not looking up at me anymore.

"Uh, yeah, I think so." My brows furrowed, not sure what he was getting at.

"Then he's fine." Paul inclined his head firmly as he shifted into his seat. "Ian wouldn't miss the Games if he was on his death bed. He's waaaay too competitive for that bullshit. Believe me, it used to drive me nuts growing up."

"Yeah, I guess..." I trailed off. I wasn't completely pacified, but I knew I wasn't going to get any more out of Paul. He knew his brother, but maybe it was because he knew him that he wasn't seeing the warning signs like I was.

Last year, Aidan had been really worried about Ian and that Dark Arts group he was joining, but Ian had assured me it wasn't a big deal. And, up until now, it hadn't been. Ian had been his usual charming, panty melting self. The only thing I could think of that had changed in the past few months was that his parents had visited. Could they have had something to do with it?

I didn't know, but the only way I was going to find out was by meeting with Mr. and Mrs. Broomstein myself. I pulled out my phone with a determined frown.

It was time to call in a favor.

Chapter 15

THE RESTAURANT I WAS supposed to meet Mrs. Broomstein at was way too classy for my style. There was a dress code that required me to not only to wear a dress, but also a pointed hat like some kind of fairy-tale witch. The wait staff hovered above the floor as they sat the guests. Even the floating plates that came out of the back room on their own had an air of refinement and judgment to them. I watched from where I waited at the hostess stand as a plate of pasta flew off the table before the lady eating it could take another bite.

"Hey, I was eating that," the plump woman cried out, her fork midair.

The plate paused in the air and the noodles formed a mouth twisted in a disgusted frown. "And everything else in the house it seems," the dish snapped back.

The woman gasped and placed a hand on her chest, her brows bunching down in the middle. "Why I never!"

"Are you sure this is the place?" I asked my grandmother, Nina. The only way I'd been able to get Mrs. Broomstein to meet with me was to have my grandmother request to have lunch with her. Mrs. Broomstein didn't even know I was coming, something I hoped wouldn't be a problem since it had to do with her son and not me.

My grandmother looked up from her phone and glanced around the room, not at all bothered by any of the horrible aspects of the restaurant. "Yes, I'm sure. The Broomsteins have a regular table here."

I crossed my arms and glowered. "Of course they do."

"Maxine, I'm not sure what you are hoping to accomplish with this meeting. Willow Broomstein is not the kind of person who would..." She trailed off, her face pinched as if she weren't sure what to say.

I let out a huff and adjusted my hat. "The kind of person who would like me? That's what you were going to say, right?"

My grandmother sighed and tucked her phone back into her pale mint green purse. It matched quite well with the skirt and blouse she wore. "I understand your concern for their son, but he is an adult, one that has made it clear he wants nothing to do with his parents or the society we have put so much effort into."

"I don't care. It's not about that. He's their son, something is wrong, and it all started with them." I scowled and stomped my foot in place, determined to get to the bottom of it.

"I would say that we do have a problem," a cool and collected voice commented from behind us.

I slowly turned to meet the same mesmerizing green and brown eyes that I had come to love on the face of a dark-haired woman about my mother's age. Mrs. Broomstein wore a form-fitting dress of a cream color that was probably the height of fashion somewhere, probably Milan or something.

Me, I liked my clothes to cost less than my car. At least, I knew I'd never outgrow my car, but a pair of pants? That was something else.

"Mrs. Broomstein." I beamed at her as I offered her my hand. "It's so great to finally meet you. Ian and Paul have told me so much about you. I feel like I know you already." I laid the compliments on thick, hoping to kill any dislike she had for me with kindness.

Mrs. Broomstein sniffed and withdrew her hand, staring at it as if she had just touched the trash. "I highly doubt that. My sons and I have a tenuous relationship if anything. I doubt they would talk about me unless under severe torture."

I forced a smile and let out a nervous laugh. "Uh, yeah. Okay."

"Willow, how lovely to see you." My grandmother came to the rescue, air-kissing the sides of Willow's face. "We haven't had a proper meal together since that last dinner during the harvest moon. I was so sad to hear you couldn't come to Maxine's coming out party. We missed you."

Willow let out a long sigh and rubbed her temples. "Yes. Well, Tylus's work is keeping us on our toes this year. I've seemed to have missed quite a few new developments." Her eyes narrowed on me as she spoke. I didn't need to be psychic to know she didn't like me, not that I knew why. I hadn't done anything other than exist, but I'd learned already in this world that was a crime enough.

Thankfully, before either my grandmother or myself could make matters worse, the hostess appeared. "Is everyone in the party here?"

"Yes," I said while Mrs. Broomstein said, "No."

My grandmother was the one to question her. "No? Who else are we waiting for?"

Just then the door opened to reveal a familiar redhead clad in a dress similar to Willow's, her own little pointed hat pinned fashionably to the side of her curled hair.

"Sorry, I'm late," Beth Ann cooed. "Y'all wouldn't imagine the traffic on the way here. Y'all'd think there'd be a broom network or at least a teleportation station around these parts."

"Yes, well, we do with what we have," Willow mused before air-kissing Beth Ann's face and bringing her into our little group. I tried to keep the hatred off my face, but I'd never been good at pretending and probably ended up looking constipated more than anything.

"Beth Ann," I gritted out as the hostess directed us to our seats. "I didn't know you were coming."

"Willow invited me." Beth Ann beamed over her shoulder at me before taking her seat at the round table the hostess directed us to. We took our respective seats with me between my grandmother and Beth Ann, and Willow across from me. I picked up my menu and tried to distract my annoyance with the words on the page, but it wasn't easy.

The table had a pale pink tablecloth with so many utensils around the plate settings that I was thankful my grandmother had given me a lesson back at my coming out party. The centerpiece, of course, couldn't be anything normal. It was made up of twigs and feathers with some kind of exotic fruit and flowers.

"When you said you wanted to meet for lunch, Nina, I figured it would be a good as time as any to see my darling Beth Ann." Willow reached over and patted Beth Ann's hand. "You know we used to be close friends with her parents. That's until they moved to Houston."

"Yes, I'm aware." My grandmother took it in stride with a pleasant expression. "How are your parents, Beth Ann?"

Beth Ann lowered her menu and gazed happily at my grandmother. "They're doing well, thank you for askin'. How is Mr. Mancaster? Has his arthritis cleared up?"

"Arthritis?" I shot a look at my grandmother who shifted uncomfortably in her seat. "You never told me grandfather had arthritis."

"You never asked," my grandmother huffed. "Now, what will you be eating?" She picked her menu back up as if everything wasn't going to hell in a handbasket. "I recommend the veal or a salad. I wouldn't get anything too heavy unless you want the dishes to get nasty on you."

The rest of the table laughed except me. This was not going as I planned. Not only did Beth Ann hijack my lunch with Ian and Paul's mom, but she had shared jokes and knew personal stuff about my own family that I had no idea about. If I wanted to make myself look bad in front of Mrs. Broomstein, I would have just asked her to meet at the school cafeteria. At least then I could eat a burger without getting rude comments from the dishware.

196

The waitress came by and took our orders. I'd settled for a cream of potato soup. I figured I couldn't go wrong with that, not unless the dish decided to dump it in my lap… Crap, maybe I should have just ordered a salad. Fuck. Too late now.

"So, Maxine…" Willow drawled, lifting her water glass to her mouth to take a dainty sip. "You were concerned about my son?"

I opened my mouth to explain, but Beth Ann beat me to it. "Pardon me, but for those of us not aware of the situation, which son are you talkin' about? Paul or Ian? You are dating both of them, aren't you?"

I wished with all my heart that I could blast lasers out of my eyes to incinerate Beth Ann right there in her chair. Sadly, the one time I needed my powers to go above and beyond the call of duty, they don't even flutter.

To Willow, I bit out through clenched teeth, "Ian. He's been rather distant, really not himself. The only thing I could think of was that it started just after your visit. I was wondering if you could have discussed something that might have made him upset?"

"Well, I would think so." She paused and thanked a pitcher that flew over to refill our drinks. "Ian will be graduating soon and that means he needs to think about his future. Mucking about as he has been was fine when he was a first or second year, but real life is just around the corner, and he can't keep pretending like nothing will change."

I frowned at Willow's explanation. "And what exactly has to change? Ian's studying the Dark Arts, he joined the group for it, won't he just find a job doing that?"

Beth Ann and Willow gave a small pitying laugh that made my hand curl tight around my knife. However, it was my grandmother who answered my question.

"Maxine, dear, the Dark Arts isn't something you can make a profession out of. Not unless you plan to be a scholar and rarely do any of those actually make any money. They'd have to discover something extraordinary to make the magical community want to back them." She paused and glanced over at Willow, before she continued slowly, "I believe Willow's concern is that Ian may be putting himself through a lot of future difficulties for a lost cause. It would be far more rational for him to join his father's company at this point."

"But he doesn't want that," I blurted out, just as our meals flew to our table. I waited impatiently for the plates and bowls to settle down before launching back into my argument. "Why should he give up his dream just because it isn't something you agree with? Maybe he will achieve something great, but you wouldn't know because you made him quit before he did it."

Willow let out a tired sigh. "I would be more than thrilled if my son achieved anything at this point, but Ian is determined to go against us no matter what it is." She paused and turned to Beth Ann. "Look at our lovely Beth Ann for instance. They were happily courting and well on their way to being engaged when, the moment we approved of the match, he threw it all away to focus on the Dark Arts."

Willow let out a bitter laugh. "And look where that has gotten him? In a relationship with a half witch who cannot even choose between the men in her life. It's clear he is only doing this to make sure we never approve of it." I must have had a hurt expression, because she reached across the table and patted my hand. "I don't mean to say this to be cruel, but I would be remiss if I didn't warn you. After all, your mother used to be a close friend of mine in school." She released my hand to take another sip of her glass as if she hadn't thrown several insults in my face in front of my grandmother and my nemesis.

I took several spoonfuls of my soup as I tried to gather my strength. My grandmother had a pensive look on her face, but she didn't rush to defend me. I should hate her for it, but I didn't. I knew she must be torn between sticking up for me, and what my unconventional relationship has done to her social standing. My mom hadn't even made this much of a stir, and she had married a human!

Still, it didn't keep it from stinging a little.

Regardless of my feelings, I needed to think of Ian. He was the one who was in trouble, not me. They could say what they liked. Beth Ann could sit smugly in the background for the rest of my life for all I cared, but that's where she'd stay, in the background, on the sidelines of the life she wanted with Ian but could never have. After I rallied myself, I set my spoon down with a definitive clink.

"Mrs. Broomstein, thank you for taking the time out of your busy schedule to meet with me." When she started to answer, I put my hand up. "I'm not quite finished. While I understand your concerns about the relationship between your sons and me, I want you to know that I love your sons, both of them, dearly. I will do everything in my power to make sure their dreams come true, no matter how silly and irrational they may seem to you. Seeing as your meeting could not have done anything to make Ian act the way he currently is—"

"How do you know that?" Beth Ann cut in with a smirk. "How do you know he's not distancing himself because he is finally realizin' where he belongs?"

"Because," I snapped as I stood up, my jaw set firmly, "the Ian I know wouldn't let peer pressure or any other kind of pressure keep him from doing what he wanted." A slow, wicked grin slid up my lips. "And it's like you said, Mrs. Broomstein, he lives to defy you. Why would he change that now, when he has every reason to do so?"

"We'll cut him off," Mrs. Broomstein countered... and that just made me laugh.

"Well, you go ahead with that," I said with a last giggle, "because, from where I'm standing, your money hasn't done much for Paul or Ian but make their lives miserable. I haven't had millions to live off of, and I've been perfectly happy."

Beth Ann snorted, but my grandmother looked oddly pleased by my outburst. Not to let the meal end on a low note, I smiled and gave a small curtsey, though, I had no idea why.

"Now, as I said, thank you. You have reminded me that if anything happens, I will be there for Ian, no matter what." I enunciated the last part as I stared Beth Ann down before I pushed away from the table and marched for the door. Before I got to the door, Beth Ann grabbed my elbow. I spun around and pulled away from her.

"What do you want now?"

Beth Ann had a hesitant look on her face, her teeth pulling her lower lip into her mouth. "How do you do it?"

I sighed and crossed my arms. "Do what?"

She shot a glance over her shoulder as if she might get caught talking to me. "Not worry about money or... or what people would think?"

For a second, I felt bad for Beth Ann. Like Sabrina and the rest of the privileged jerks I had run into, they only knew the world one way: follow your parents' and society's rules, or suffer the consequences. They never stopped to think for a minute what would happen if they all stopped playing along. What would happen if the magical society had to change with them?

That would be a day to remember.

I shrugged in response to her question. "It's not that I don't care what people think. It's clear that I do. I wouldn't be here trying to make nice with Mrs. Broomstein otherwise. However, I also don't let what others want me to be define me." I thought for a moment and then took a step toward her. "Just as you shouldn't marry someone just because your parents think you should."

I thought I'd gotten through to her for a moment. For just a single millisecond, a glimmer of hope appeared in Beth Ann's eyes before it was gone, and the bitch was back.

She plastered a fake smile on her lips and moved away from me.

"Well, at least we know I will always be one step above you, both with the Broomsteins and in the games. You might as well give up now before you embarrass yourself."

I sighed and shook my head before turning back to the door and ignoring her further snipes. We almost had a moment there, but I was naive to think I could win two bullies over in the span of my lifetime.

Oh well. Maybe next year.

Chapter 16

AS I STOOD BEFORE the mirror in my dorm room a few minutes before the Halloween party, I stared at my reflection and tugged at the hemline of my dress. I'd decided to go as a fairy for my Halloween costume, except I looked more like a cheap hooker than a fairy at the moment, though Aris did make me look the part of mystical creature as it bobbed around in the air behind me.

"Stop fretting. You look hot," Trina told me from across the room. She was casting a charm on Libby's bunny ears so that they twitched on her head on their own. Trina had decided to go as the wily hunter to Libby's rabbit. I didn't have the heart to tell them how morbid that was, but to each their own. They looked good together, no matter their costumes.

"I'm not fretting," I insisted, while pulling up the top of my green leaf dress. My girls were five seconds away from popping out, and that was with an adhesive charm. The bottom of the dress wasn't any better. It rode so tightly against my butt that I knew I'd be showing cheek if I dared to bend over an inch. Sighing in defeat, I threw my hands down. "I just don't think I look enough like a fairy. I mean, my wings aren't even that fairy like." I moved over to the bed where my pretend wings sat, sad and pathetic.

"That's because you didn't buy them from the right store," Sabrina scoffed from where she'd taken up residence on my bed. She looked every inch like a queen of Egypt, complete with black hair and hissing vipers wrapped around her arms. Right now, the vipers were laying in her lap as she stroked their heads. How she'd gotten them to obey her, I didn't know, but then again, they came from the same genus, so it wasn't that farfetched.

"I'm sorry, your highness. I didn't have time to go with you while I was running interference with the Broomsteins and schoolwork." I sniffed and pulled my wings onto my shoulders by the straps. They were yellow with green edges and would have looked perfect if I'd been at any other kind of school, but next to the others and their magical costumes, I wasn't even second best.

"Oh geez," Trina huffed as she moved away from Libby to my side. "Just freaking charm them for Merlin's sake. It's not rocket science."

I crossed my arms and I glanced over my shoulder at Trina where she'd begun to fiddle with my wings. "Well, you know, not all of us know how to do all that stuff. I didn't even think to charm anything until I saw you doing Libby's ears. With my luck, though, I'll end up charming the damn things into a butterfly, and I wouldn't have wings at all."

Libby giggled and murmured ditzily, "Butterflies are pretty."

"Yes, they are, baby," Trina air-kissed behind me as I rolled my eyes. Then she turned back to my wings. "Now, hold still. I just need to get them in the right position first, and then..." A warmth spread over me as Trina's magic pushed into the wings and into my back.

"Hey, what are you doing?" I asked a bit nervously. "You aren't spelling me too, are you?"

"Of course," Trina exclaimed with a snort. "They're not wings if they don't look like they're part of you. So, now, they do."

"Wow, nice spell work!" Sabrina and her vipers came up close behind me. She touched the edge of one of the wings, and I shivered from the feel of her cold fingers. "Did you feel that?"

"Yes," I squeaked, part of me scared to look in the mirror and see what Trina had actually done.

"Very nice," Sabrina announced and then added, "You know, for you."

Trina's voice was heavy with sarcasm when she replied, "Oh, thank you, mighty queen."

Unable to hold back any longer, I rushed to the mirror and stared in awe. The cheap little plastic wings I'd bought had grown and were now at least three feet in length on either side. I flexed the muscles in my back, and the wings spread out to follow. As I tested them with different movements, I was so completely engrossed by my new wings that I didn't hear the knock on the bedroom door.

"What are you doing here?" Sabrina growled, and that snapped me right out of my fascination. I looked at her through the mirror as she stood by the door, her hand on her hip and the other holding one of her vipers. The person she was giving attitude to was none other than Chadwick Von Wood.

He was dressed in a pair of pants, slacks actually, a far cry from the shorts he always seemed to wear. Even more surprising was the white button-down shirt that had frills along the cuffs and neck. Chad did not look like a guy who would ever wear something that pretentious.

"Uh, hey, Sabrina. I was looking for..." Chad's eyes moved into the room to land on me. His face wasn't the usual carefree, fun-loving surfer guy that I'd learned to semi-tolerate. It was full of tension and maybe a bit of nervousness. What was that about?

"What's up, Chad?" I took Sabrina's spot by the door and waited patiently to see what the Cali wizard had to say.

Chad shoved his hands through his hair. It was messed up even more than usual, as if he'd been doing this for hours straight rather than throughout the day. He shoved his hands into his pockets and kind of ducked his head, a sheepish grin on his lips.

"Hey, Max. Have you talked to Callie lately?"

I cocked my head to the side and glanced at Trina who only shrugged. "Uh, yeah. Why?" I shifted one hip to the side, my arms crossing under my breasts. What did Beth Ann's fiancé want with my best friend?

"So, did she tell you that she was my date for tonight's party?" Chad asked.

I made a choking sound as my eyes bugged from my head. "She what?"

Sabrina snickered behind me. "Oh, man, tonight is going to be fun."

"No." I shot her a quiet look before turning back to Chad. "Callie didn't tell me."

"Wonder why...?" Sabrina muttered under her breath, and I ignored her.

"Well..." Chad hesitated, and then a bit more determined, continued, "She is. My date, that is. And I was hoping you'd maybe help me keep her away from Beth Ann?"

Sabrina threw her head back and laughed hysterically. "You might as well wish for a million dollars because that is as likely to happen as what you're asking."

I arched a brow and jutted my chin in Sabrina's direction. "What she said."

"Come on, please." Chad clasped his hands in front of him as he begged. "I really like Callie. She's not like the other women I know…"

"You mean, she's not a witch," I inserted, getting a bit defensive of my bestie. So what if she didn't tell me she and Chad had started talking? Or that they were going to the party together? That didn't stop her from being my best friend. It's not like I told her everything either. However, I would think she'd have told me about this one. It was quite a doozy.

"Well, yeah." Chad dragged his hand through his hair again and then shrugged. "But it's not just that. She's so cool. She knows so much. Like, important stuff. It's not all about getting married and finding the right magical china pattern with her."

"How long have you guys been talking exactly?" I couldn't help but ask. I needed to know what I was dealing with here. Were they just talking good fun in a flirty non-serious kind of way? Or were they talking in more of an 'I want to be around you and no one else' kind of way? Seeing as Callie hadn't mentioned him to me once in the last few months, I was hoping for the first one.

Chad took a deep breath and let it out slowly. "Since the welcome party."

"You guys have been talking for that long?" My mouth dropped open, and I blinked several times to get my mind to reactivate. "Why am I just hearing about it?"

Trina came up beside me and wrapped an arm around my shoulder to give me a tight hug. "Maybe she was insecure about what it might become."

"Or she was ashamed of Chadwick Von Wood," Sabrina unhelpfully supplied. "He's a walking dick joke waiting to happen. Besides, he's not exactly serious boyfriend material."

"Hello, the walking dick joke is still here?" Chad waved a hand with a scowl. "Damn, Sabrina, you really know how to let a guy have it."

Sabrina lifted a shoulder, a bored expression on her face. "I just tell it how I see it, Von Wood."

"Anyway, that's off topic." I waved my hands between them to break up their little snit. "Chad, why aren't you taking Beth Ann?"

Chad snorted. "Look, Beth Ann and I might be engaged by our parents' standards, but she doesn't want anything to do with me. Man, she already had a date when I asked

Callie." He shrugged his shoulders. "So, I figured that I was a free agent."

Sabrina barked a laugh. "Ha. No such thing with Beth Ann."

"Right." I pointed at Sabrina and narrowed a look at Chad. "I have to agree with Sabrina on this one. You are here trying to get me to keep your would-be fiancée away from your... girlfriend? Are you two boyfriend/girlfriend?"

"I don't know." Chad gave me a goofy kind of grin. "I was gonna ask her tonight."

"You do know Beth Ann is going to blow a gasket." Sabrina mimed an explosion with her hands and mouth. "I mean, nuclear. Not just because you are bringing someone else, because obviously, she's doing the same, but because you're bringing a human and that said human is besties with her competition. Not that she even has a chance in hell with Ian."

I gave Sabrina a grateful smile before turning back to Chad. "Look, I want what is best for Callie. If she wants to be with you, fine, but you have to be able to stand up to Beth Ann. You know as well as I do that, without magic, Callie is a sitting duck for Beth Ann's torment, and I'm not about to have that happen. If you can't promise me that you'll protect her, you won't be dating her long." I paused for dramatic effect. "So, can you protect her?"

Chad's face grew serious, his eyes hardened, and his lips pressed into a thin, straight line. With a jerk of his chin, and without any hint of that fun loving guy in there, Chad stated, "With my life."

"Good." I patted Chad on the chest. "Then we won't have a problem."

Chad sagged as if being serious for that long had taken a lot out of him. He gave me a lopsided grin. "Thanks, Max. So, I'll see ya there?"

"Looks like it." I grinned at him. Chad waved a hand at the rest of them and I closed the door behind me. When the door was firmly closed, I rushed over to my desk and snatched up my phone to rapidly type out a text to Callie.

Me: When were you going to tell me you were dating Chadwick Von Wood?????

"I hope you know that tonight is going to be a disaster." Sabrina glanced over my shoulder as I typed another message to Callie when she didn't immediately answer.

I glowered in her direction. "I am aware, thank you, Queen Obvious."

"I'm just saying... Beth Ann already hates you because of Ian, but now, your human friend is dating her fiancé?" Sabrina huffed a laugh as she adjusted her sheer white dress so that it didn't show so much side boob. "If you're not dead meat, then Callie certainly is."

"I'm not going to let that happen," I snapped back, clutching my phone tightly in my hand.

"You mean that *we* aren't." Trina moved to stand beside me with a lethal grin.

"No, honey." Libby took Trina's arm with a frown. "That's wrong. Max isn't more than one person."

Trina and I exchanged a look before Trina took Libby's hand. "I mean, we are going to help her keep Callie safe."

"Oh." Libby's eyes widened as her mouth formed a large o-shape. Nodding enthusiastically, she grinned. "Oh, yeah. Definitely. That's what friends do, even if they are just humans."

I rolled my eyes and held back a laugh. I couldn't fault the girl. It just wouldn't be fair. "Thanks, Libby." To the rest of them, I clasped my hands together. "So, are we ready?"

Before any of them could answer, another knock came sounded on my dorm room door. I sighed and marched over to it, muttering, "I swear, if this is another wizard wanting to date someone I'm friends with, I'm going to hex them. I'm at my quota today."

"How about a boyfriend looking to pick up his gorgeous girlfriend?" Ian answered as I opened the door. Looking sexy as all get out as a fairy prince in a pair of light green pants and a leaf-covered vest, along with his own pair of charmed wings—Ian defined the word lickable.

"Hey," I breathed, unable to rip my eyes away from his delectable abs as he leaned against the doorframe. He looked good, a lot better than the last few weeks for sure. The dark circles under his eyes were gone, and he actually seemed like he wanted to be here. I hadn't even had a chance to talk to him about lunch with his mom and Beth Ann this past week, and it looked like I might not even need to.

"If you keep eye fucking him like that, some of us are gonna need protection for the backlash," Sabrina joked without a hint of animosity.

At her words, I shook my head and beamed up at Ian. "You look great."

"So do you." Ian leaned down and kissed me on the lips, careful not to mess up my makeup. "The others are waiting in the quad. Didn't think there was enough room for all of our wings in this hallway."

"Hold up!" Sabrina jumped off the bed and scowled. "You're saying all four of you dressed up like flouncy fairy princes with wings for her?" Sabrina threw a hand in my direction, all pretense of friendship gone. There was the Sabrina I knew. Pouting as she crossed her arms, Sabrina sulked, "I couldn't even get Paul to wear matching costumes, let alone girly ones like this."

"Hey!" Ian protested as he flexed his biceps. "Does any part of this look girly?"

My eyes trailed over his form before lingering in a few places longer than appropriate. I licked my lips and murmured, "Not from where I'm standing."

Ian laughed and drew me out into the hallway. "As I said, not girly." He winked over my shoulder at Sabrina and the others before offering me his arm. "Shall we?"

I nodded eagerly. My fingers curled around his warm bicep, and I swore he flexed just a bit more for my benefit. I didn't care, I loved every second of it.

"See you down there, girls," I called over my shoulder, only half paying them any mind. My head was full of what the others would look like. If Ian was this hot like a fairy, the others had to be a wet dream combined, one that I planned to reenact in reality the moment I could.

As if the universe declared it needed something to ruin my night, my phone dinged in my hand, reminding me of the impending doom tonight's party would entail. I groaned at the text from Callie.

Callie: I didn't know how you'd react.

"Callie's dating Chad?" Ian asked as he caught sight of that and my last text.

I groaned and shoved the phone into the lone pocket of my leafy dress. "Yes, and no, I didn't know until like ten minutes ago when

Chad showed up at my door, wanting help keeping Beth Ann away."

Ian snort laughed. "Oh, yeah. That's not going to happen. They might as well hide out in his room or on another planet, because there is no way Beth Ann is going to let this go."

"That's what I said!" I screeched as my shoulders bunched up around me. My wings smacked into his, and for a second, a tiny thrill went through me. Interesting.

"So, what's the plan?" Ian moved us to the side so a few students could pass, our wings lowering on their own to make room. I think I could get used to this. Not that I needed another new thing in my life right now, but if I could learn to fly with them? That would be badass. Forget the broom. Wings were in!

I sighed and hugged his arm closer. "The plan is to have fun and not let Beth Ann kill Callie. Chad swears that he had it under control but..."

"You're a worrier, I know." Ian tugged on one of the blonde curls I had piled on my head. "Don't worry. If all five of us, plus Chad, can't keep Beth Ann at bay, no one can."

"Plus Libby and Trina," I pointed out before I frowned. "Maybe Sabrina... but I have a feeling she'd be happier standing on the sidelines cheering as it all goes up in smoke."

Ian chuckled as he inclined his head. "Yeah, that's her. She and my mom have something in common there."

The fact that Ian brought up his mom made me stop walking. Ian pulled back, his brows furrowing. "What's wrong?"

"About your mom…" I chewed on my lower lip with a nervous smile. "I had lunch with her this week."

"You did?" Ian arched a brow, a hint of a smile on his lips. "How did that turn out?"

I groaned, and Ian laughed.

"That good, huh?"

"Worse." I rolled my eyes. "Beth Ann showed up with her."

Ian let out a bitter laugh. "Not surprising. She's the only person who was further up my parents' ass than Sabrina."

I waited for him to ask what we talked about, but he didn't. I wasn't sure if that was because of disinterest or that he was utterly unworried about what might have happened.

"Don't you want to know what we talked about?" I asked at last.

Ian gave me a sideways look. "You mean besides me?"

My brows shot up to my forehead. "You knew?"

"I know that I've not been myself lately," Ian bobbed his head, his eyes facing forward, "but I'm alright now."

He didn't elaborate more, and I couldn't leave well enough alone.

"And the reason you weren't yourself was because of what your parents said, right?"

A tiny smile crept up Ian's lips. "You could say that. I want to be sure I make something of myself in the Dark Arts, and the only way I'm going to do that is do something that no one else has been able to do."

"And have you done it?" I was curious to know what he could do in the Dark Arts that was groundbreaking. The name of the art itself wasn't very enlightening, and I feared what he could be getting into that would keep him so run down.

Ian patted my hand as we moved close enough to the quad that the music pouring out made it harder to hear him. "Not yet, but I'm close."

As Ian pulled me into the horde of costumed students, he didn't say anything else about it. I quickly forgot all about it too, because the decor was everything I had hoped for and more by a Halloween party run by witches and wizards. Bubbles floated through the air, and streams of sparkling light flew by and danced in my hair, making me giggle. Pumpkins carved with faces shifted their expressions and talked to the students passing by on their own.

If the quad wasn't already a haunted wonderland, all of the students dressed up like goblins, fairies, and the like would have tipped it off. Someone had even cast a spell on them so they were as small as hobbits! Now that was dedication.

We passed by the refreshment table where jelly eyeballs watched you as you passed and sausage fingers waved hello. There were gummy spiders that tried to get away as you reached for them and smoking drinks that really gave them the spooky witch feeling.

The event team had really gone all out for this event. I'd have to tell Dale what a good job they did when I saw him.

Even the floor was charmed with smoke and zombie hands shooting up from the floor. One of them came up beside me and I shrieked, jumping away from it and closer to Ian.

"They won't touch you," Ian shouted in my ear over the music as he wrapped his arms around my waist. "Too much of a liability."

"Why have them then?" I asked, relaxing a bit as I watched the hand I'd jumped away from pretend to grab someone else, but never quite touching them.

Instead of Ian answering, Dale appeared from the crowd, decked out in a rose-colored outfit similar to Ian's and said, "Where's the fun in that?"

"Some of us aren't psychos who like to be scared for fun." I grinned as I approached him and wrapped my arms around his waist.

"This is so great. I can't believe you did all this."

"Thanks, it wasn't just m,e but I think it came together okay."

I snorted. "You don't give yourself enough credit. And by the way..." My gaze moved over his costume, appreciating the way his outfit showed all the best aspects of him. He had run some product through his wily auburn hair and that, paired with his glasses, caused a warmth to burn low between my thighs. "You look good."

After he pressed a kiss to my lips that left me gasping, Dale stroked the skin below the line of my dress. "So do you. Wings become you."

"You too." My eyes drifted to his wings, a matching pair of emerald green ones folded close to his body. It seemed everyone knew to get charmed wings but me. "Where are the others?"

"Here." Paul pushed through the crowd with Aidan close on his heels. Paul looked just as delicious as Ian, but in a more princely manner than his bad boy brother. His eyes twinkled in the magical lighting, and his hair fell into his face where he kept pushing it back. The wings on his back were pale blue and flickered a darker tint every so often to match his pants and top.

"Oh, my." My hand came up to my mouth to hide the grin I couldn't hold back as I took in Aidan's appearance. If there was one guy on campus who shouldn't have dressed as a fairy, it was my large, masculine boyfriend Aidan. While his clothes fit him perfectly and the red wings were just like the others, he looked downright ridiculous in an adorably cute way. He had a flat expression on his face as if he couldn't decide if he liked or hated what he was wearing, but had just given into it.

Unable to help myself, I poked at his bare abs. "So, what do you think of the wings? Think they'd be more fun than a broom?"

Aidan flexed his wings and then, with a thoughtful expression, grunted, "Not big enough."

"Not big enough?" I laughed. "They're already like six feet wide. I'm having issues not running into anyone."

Shaking his head, Aidan held his hands out to measure. "The weight to size ratio is off. They wouldn't hold me." His eyes skimmed over my form, making me flush. "Maybe you."

I giggled, pleased, and let my hands play on his abs for a moment before my eyes caught onto a familiar dark head of hair. I turned to get a good luck at Callie, and my mouth dropped open and my eyes widened at the pink Renaissance dress covering my best friend's body.

"Callie!" I called out over the music, and my bestie turned from where she was giggling at Chad to me. For a second, guilt covered her face, but then she plastered a smile on, lifted her skirts, and hurried toward me. Chad quickly followed, much to my surprise. His eyes moved with her, a smile never too far from his lips, even as he kept checking around the room nervously, no doubt looking for Beth Ann.

"Max, you look... Wow!" Callie clasped my arms with her hands and took in my whole outfit. "This is so cool." She focused on my fairy wings. "Are those real?"

I lifted a shoulder and grinned. "For the night. What about you?" I let my eyes roam over the petticoats and bows of her dress, admiring the way her waist looked so tiny. I bet that corset was a bitch to put on. "Why didn't you come over and get ready? I would have helped you." I let out a small pout and stomp of my foot.

Callie smiled shyly at Chad. "I didn't know what to say..."

"Yo, Broomstein... es, Templar, Varnes!" Chad nodded to each of my guys, shaking a few of their hands and blowing up fists like they were old buddies. A chorus of 'Von Wood's' was returned before they started to talk about the upcoming Game, a broom race from what I could overhear.

It was an event I still wasn't sure I would even be participating in. I still hadn't gotten much better at keeping my shit together broom riding after the first class, even with Aidan there to hold my hand. I pushed that thought aside as I focused on Callie. I looped my arm with hers and pulled her to the side, so we had some privacy.

"You could have just told me, you know," I said quietly. "I wouldn't have judged. Besides, Beth Ann obviously doesn't give a rat's ass about Chad, who seems like a good guy by the way. That witch keeps trying to shove her way into Ian's life even if she's not dating him." And when I said witch, I really meant bitch. That woman was winning no personality awards here.

Callie chewed on her lower lip to try to hold back a dreamy smile. "Yeah, he kind of is, isn't he? Beth Ann can kiss my perfectly sculpted ass. Chad told me all about their arranged marriage and how he wasn't even their first choice." he growled and sniffed, her eyes locking onto someone behind me. "Like she has any right to be that picky. She couldn't tell a real man if he kissed her on her phony ass."

I chuckled and mock hissed. "Me-ow. Someone's jealous."

"Not jealous." Callie put her nose in the air. "Determined. I won't let Beth Ann and her parents ruin what could possibly be something real for Chad and me." She paused and squirmed for a moment. "Even if we're ill-matched."

"Why would you even think that?" I scoffed. "Ill-matched. He should be so lucky." I threw Chad a vicious look that he frowned at but didn't ask about.

Callie shifted in place. "Well, I am a human. He's a wizard."

"So?"

With an exasperated sigh, Callie groaned, "People will talk."

Before I could get a word out to counter her, a whiff of evil floated by. Oh, wait! That was just Beth Ann.

"What in tarnation is she doing here?" Beth Ann's usual Southern drawl was filled with venom. She had decided to go as a harpy, extremely appropriate, including a barely there crimson dress that clung to her tinted red skin, and a pair of feathery demon-like wings. Her tongue forked out when she hissed in Callie's direction.

I moved to interpose myself between my friend and the witch, but before I could even say a word, Chad was there. He slid his arm around Callie's waist and pulled her close to his side with a lopsided grin on his lips.

"Callie's here with me," he pronounced. "As my date."

"No, she's not!" Beth Ann snapped, glaring at Chad as if that settled everything. "Get rid of her."

I felt my magic start to fester and writhe at Beth Ann's blatant dismissal of my best friend in the world. I prepared for an all-out magical brawl like I'd had with Sabrina first semester, but it turned out that there wasn't any need. Before the first spell could get thrown, Chad locked eyes with her, his grin never leaving his face, as he faced Beth Ann down.

"No way. Don't you have your own date to attend to?" He jerked his head in the direction of the confused and a bit uncomfortable male dressed in a similar fashion to Beth Ann with matching wings, but with a pair of pants painted to his lower half rather than a dress.

Beth Ann barely gave her date a second glance before turning to Callie with a sickly-sweet smile. "You don't want to do this, human. It won't turn out well for you."

Callie, fierce woman that she was, never so much as batted an eyelash as she came toe to toe with the wicked witch of Texas. "Oh, I think I do, witch." Except like me, she really didn't mean witch that way.

I couldn't hold back my glee and wanted to see the prissy redhead put in her place. As I looked on, a large hand landed on my shoulder, and I didn't have to look up to know it was Aidan at my back. The other guys gathered around us as well to show a united force against Beth Ann and her bitchery.

Beth Ann didn't flinch at Callie's statement. Instead, the witch placed her hand on Callie's arm, her eyes peering down at the dress with suspicious interest. "This is such a gorgeous costume. I bet you had to wear quite the corset to get into it, didn't you?" As she said the words, her eyes tightened at the edges.

Callie opened her mouth to retort, but her words came out as a sudden gasp for breath. She grabbed at Beth Ann's hand, her panicked eyes jerking from her to me to Chad and back. It took me longer than I liked to admit to before I realized that Beth Ann was casting a hex... but not Ian.

"That's crossing the line, Beth Ann!" Ian clamped his hand down on Beth Ann's arm, his eyes hard on the redhead's face. "Let her go."

"Fine, but the human needs to know who she's dealin' with." Beth Ann pretended to pout and then with a little shrug, released Callie from her spell. Callie gasped and fell into Chad's arms where he was more than ready to comfort her, his face no longer smiling as his eyes shot daggers in Beth Ann's direction.

No longer able to stand on the sidelines, I stepped into Beth Ann's personal space. "That human has a name—Callie. And I don't think you know who you are dealing with, bitch." I dropped all pretenses of being nice and let my magic crackle along my arms and into my hands, a clear show to the Bluebonnet that I had no problem throwing down right then and there.

"Now, now, save it for the Games," one of the chaperones, Headmaster Swordson, tutted at us as he stepped into our little group. He glanced down at my hands and arched a brow at me. "Miss Mancaster?"

With a reluctant growl, I released the magic back into myself but didn't move my gaze from Beth Ann's. I tightened my jaw and bit out, "You can count on that. Looks like I just joined tomorrow's race."

"You don't want to do that," Beth Ann jeered, flipping her hair over her shoulder. "You'll just embarrass yourself and your human."

"I bet you."

Beth Ann crossed her arms over her chest and arched a brow. "Bet me what?"

I stepped closer so that I was inches away from Beth Ann's face and shoved a finger at her chest. "If I win, you lay off of Callie."

"And if I win?" Beth Ann turned her face to the side, pretending to examine her nails. "What do I get?"

I thought about it for a second and then looked to Ian. "I'll break up with Ian."

Ian scoffed and shook his head but didn't argue. It was nice to know he trusted me. I had no plans on letting Beth Ann win. Nor did I have any plans on breaking up with Ian, at least not permanently. Loopholes, you know?

A slow, evil grin slid up Beth Ann's face. "Why I would be happier than a dead pig in the sunshine."

I glanced over at the others, wondering if they had any clue about what Beth Ann had just said, but then the redhead sighed with annoyance.

"Yes. That's a yes, darling."

I held my hand out for her to shake. "Then we have a deal."

Beth Ann gave my hand a little disgusted look before reluctantly shaking it. "Deal. Y'all are going to regret this more than a harlot going to Sunday school."

Now, I couldn't disagree with that one.

Chapter 17

THE DAY OF THE first game was the perfect weather for broom flying—clear skies and not a single rain cloud in the sky. There was even a cool breeze fluttering my hair as I waited near the bleachers of the athletic field for the MagiX Games to start.

They had transformed the athletic field into something I'd only seen in the movies or on television. Long poles stuck out of the ground all along the sides of the field, each with a different school's emblem and name on them. Stations with drinks and concessions were set up for the spectators to buy. They were even selling little flying brooms and miniature school flags so you could cheer your team on.

The bleachers were already filled with tons of witches and wizards waiting to watch the first game of the year. Callie sat with my parents and grandparents, determined to cheer Chad on regardless of the threat from Beth Ann. They had already planned on coming, but after finding out that I was participating, they were overjoyed to cheer me on.

The field already had a bunch of students from all the schools preparing with their brooms for the big race. Of course, this couldn't just be a regular old race, like flying in a straight line or anything simple like that. No, it had to be an obstacle course with loops and turns and weaving back and forth, going from three feet above the ground to fifty feet. It was enough to make anyone think twice about entering.

Including me.

I wasn't ashamed to admit that I was nervous, really nervous. I hadn't been this nervous since the first day of school. My hands were sweating, my stomach was doing a somersault, and—

"Are you sure you want to do this?" Dale touched my elbow, making me jump in place.

I swallowed several times as I tried to push back the urge to hurl. Eventually getting myself under control, I nodded my head a few times in quick succession before I turned to face him.

"Yeah, I think so. I mean, I have to for Callie. It's just all so…" And Ian. But I didn't say that part.

"Stressful?" Dale supplied with a sympathetic frown.

I replied with a weak smile. "I was going to go with complicated, but yeah, let's go with that." I let out a little laugh that really only made my stomach roll. "Oh, God. I'm going to be sick."

Before I actually threw up, I rushed away from Dale and headed for the locker room. Aris flew in behind me but didn't show any signs of distress or warnings of danger. I didn't know exactly how it decided if something was dangerous or not, but apparently, my panicking wasn't enough for it.

As soon as I found a trash can, I threw up the small amount of food I'd been able to get down this morning. A moment later, a cool, soothing hand touched the back of my neck, followed by a wet cloth. I leaned back to see a worried Dale there, holding out another washcloth with his free hand. I gladly accepted it to wipe my mouth clean.

"Thanks," I gasped, and then grimaced. "Ugh. Man, that must have been attractive."

"Don't worry about it. It happens to the best of us." Dale gave a small smile and then handed me a glass of water he conjured out of thin air.

"You're so good at that." I took a sip before handing it back to him.

"Thanks," he said humbly.

With that, the glass disappeared, and a toothbrush replaced it, already topped with toothpaste. With a giggle, I took the brush and headed to the sink. "It's like you read my mind."

Dale lifted a shoulder and dropped it. "The only thing worse than throwing up is having to deal with the yucky aftertaste."

"Yucky?" I asked around my toothbrush, so my words came out garbled. "Really?"

Shoving his glasses up his nose, Dale shrugged. "It's a technical term. Very sophisticated."

"I see." I spit and rinsed my mouth in the sink of the locker room. As I turned to lean on the counter, I cocked my head to the side. "And what else would you recommend, Doctor Dale?"

"For the nerves?" Dale grinned as he sauntered across the room to stand before me, his hands finding their way to either side of the sink to trap me between him and it. "I'd say the best thing for nerves is a big, fat d—"

"Don't you dare say dick." I giggled and shoved him back.

Dale smirked. "I was going to say diversion, but it's the same thing, I guess."

I shook my head, unable to stop grinning, and walked toward him. "We don't have time for that kind of diversion. The race will start any minute now."

"Not if we're quick," Dale cajoled, his hands sliding around my waist to cup my butt before pushing me up against the hardness beneath his pants.

Since we were riding brooms, the outfits were a bit different than for Potion Ball. It was all about aerodynamics, which meant slicked-back hair, fitted clothes, and every inch of you on display beneath the form-fitting material.

"I don't think I can get in and out of these things that fast," I countered, while my hands moved over the front of his pants to grip him in my palm.

Moving his hips against my ministrations, Dale groaned, before murmuring, "That's what magic is for."

"But someone could see." I pressed a kiss to his neck and then another to the line of his jaw.

Dale's fingers dipped between my thighs and stroked me through the fabric. "Do you really care?"

I gasped and spread my legs farther for him. "Not really, but I—"

The locker room door opened with a loud bang, and we quickly jumped away from one another, Dale's face turning redder than my own. God, was he adorable. A gaggle of female students came in, chattering on their way to the bathroom, all hyped up for the race.

Dale and I were quiet until they moved into the locker room, not paying us much mind.

It was a unisex locker room, after all. They had charms of all kinds to prevent assault and the like. If only the human world could solve issues that easily.

"We better get back out there." Dale thumbed toward the door.

I arched a brow. "You think?"

We made our way back outside and walked over to where the students of Winchester Academy were hanging out. The only reason I'd gotten in was because I was taking the class and Aidan had vouched for me, something I think he might regret by the end of the day.

"There you are." Paul turned from where he was fiddling with his broom to Dale and me. "I've been looking for you."

I gave him a quick kiss before looking around for Ian and Aidan. The latter was with Coach Heathers, nodding his head solemnly as the Scottish coach went on about something or other. The other wizard I was looking for was nowhere to be found.

"Where's Ian?" I asked with a frown.

Paul shook his head. "I have no idea. I haven't seen him. I tried his cell, but no answer. He's still signed up, but at this rate, we might as well assume he's not coming."

My pulse fluttered, and all the nerves I'd just gotten rid of came roaring back. I jerked my head from side to side, searching for my favorite bad boy.

"He could still show," I began. "They haven't even blown the..." A high-pitched squeal filled the air, making me groan. "Whistle yet." I chewed on my lower lip and kicked the ground in frustration. "Well, damn. Where is he?"

"Maybe he had cold feet?" Dale inserted with a waggle of his eyebrows. I flushed and told my libido to pick a better time to get hot and bothered, not when I was about to have a piece of wood between my thighs and not in a good way.

"No way," Paul scoffed and shook his head. "Ian lives for this shit. He's been broom racing since he was able to get on a broom, which he never stops reminding me was at the tender age of five."

I frowned. "How old were you?"

Paul's mouth tightened at the edges. "Nine."

My lips twitched. "That's still really impressive, Paul. You know how old I was when I first got on a broom."

Paul's eyes narrowed. "That doesn't count. Special circumstances."

"I was seven," Dale supplied unhelpfully.

"See?" I pointed to Dale. "Not everyone is a prodigy broom racer." I turned to shout at the large wizard finally on his way over from Coach Heathers. "Aidan, how old were you when you first got on a broom?"

"Four."

Paul groaned and turned away from us all. Shaking my head, I stared up at Aidan. "You really need to read the room... or the field. Or whatever. Anyway, have you seen your best bud, Ian?"

Aidan shifted, his eyes flickering to the side. "No."

He's lying. Why was he lying? Aidan never lied to me. Well, the few sentences he ever got out didn't seem like lies.

"Aidan?" I shifted closer to him as the group around us started to gather to watch the beginning of the races.

One student from each school lined up to race. The race pairings were supposed to be completely random, but when they put up the list of groups, I was conveniently in the same one as Beth Ann.

I didn't believe in coincidences.

"Aidan," I said again, ignoring the race completely to focus on the man before me. "Where's Ian?"

Aidan crossed his large biceps over his chest, keeping his eyes on the broom racing as he grunted out, "Not here."

"Hello, Captain Obvious." I smacked him on the arm with a scowl. "Where is he? He's supposed to race today."

"He's not racing."

Letting out a low growl, I flicked my eyes to Dale and Paul, who didn't give me anything helpful to go on. "Why not?"

Showing the first sign of frustration, Aidan clipped, "He's busy."

"Too busy to be here and race? He loves broom racing." I gaped at Aidan and then gestured at Paul. "Even Paul said so with the five-year-old prodigy stuff. What could be more important than this?"

Aidan didn't have the chance to answer me before Coach Heathers was calling my name. Hyped up and aggravated by the non-answers I got from Aidan, I grabbed my broom and marched onto the field. I stood at the line they instructed me to and groaned at my bad luck. Of course, they would stick me right next to the she-bitch.

"Are you ready to lose, half breed?" Beth Ann chirped, looking fierce in her pale blue and black outfit similar to my own.

"To you?" I barked a laugh. "Get real."

"Have you ever even ridden a broom before?" Beth Ann mused in that heavy Southern accent of hers. "I bet you won't last two seconds out there."

"I'll last longer than you," I shot back, just before the referee gave us the signal to get ready to race. We mounted our brooms, and my hands tightened around the handle as I listened for the signal to go.

Then the whistle blew.

I kicked up my feet and pushed my magic into the broom, urging it forward. I was a bit slower on the get-go than the others, but once I was up, my magic had more pep than I expected. My fingers gripped my broom until they ached and turned white at the knuckles as I maneuvered around the first set of the obstacles. I whipped around a barrier and over the top of another. In the process, I shot past a couple of other students from the other schools, but Beth Ann was still farther ahead of me.

I gritted my teeth and pumped even more of my magic into my broom, pushing it to go faster. The next set of the obstacles moved up in the air. These consisted of several hoops set up to hover magically in the air at different heights. The goal was to fly through each of them before moving past. If you didn't get it just right, you had to go back and grab the ones you missed, which destroyed your momentum and killed any chance of winning.

That was how I bypassed the girl from Cali on my way through as she missed a hoop and had to spin back around.

As if the setup crew weren't being creative enough, they had to do another set of hoops, but this time, they moved. All five hoops swept in predictable horizontal and vertical lines through the air.

I could see Beth Ann's red hair now, just a hoop or two ahead of me. She shot a look behind her as I went through the next hoop. Then, just as I was ready to go through the next one, the hoop suddenly broke its pattern and went the completely wrong direction. I had to pull back on my broom sharply to stop myself from going past it and barely switched direction, clipping the side of the hoop on my way through.

I wasn't sure how she did it, but I was certain that Beth Ann was the cause. Scowling at the cheating witch, I pushed even faster and hurtled past the last student from one of the other schools, leaving only Beth Ann ahead of me.

As I crept up on her tail, we came upon the final challenge. This one consisted of a barrage of levitating balls that rocketed at every flyer from all directions. You either had to dodge them on your way to the finish line, or get knocked clean off your broom and out of the competition.

Beth Ann dodged through the onslaught like some kind of mermaid on a broom, sweeping through the air like she was born to be there. Me, I just poured on the magic, pulling up that intense ball of light inside my chest and pressing it into the broom. The entire thing began to vibrate as I shoved through the balls with eagerness and determination I'd never felt before.

I had to beat Beth Ann. Not only for Ian and me, but for Callie. Beth Ann couldn't win this. She wouldn't win this.

As I zoomed past a ball, another one that had been nowhere near me flew in my direction. I did a quick tuck and turn to miss it just in time. I suspected Beth Ann had a hand in that, but didn't have the time to contemplate it before I was having to dodge another one.

Beth Ann and I were neck and neck at the end of the final obstacle, even though Beth Ann had been cheating the majority of the time. I couldn't prove it of course, but it would make winning all that much sweeter.

The last stretch of the race was a straight-up rush to the bottom where the finish line waited. The plunge would put us at breakneck speeds, gravity helping our magic along, and I had to be quick to pull up in time or else I would smash into the field just before the finish line. My heart raced and fear rose in my throat, but when Beth Ann's cackling laughter hit my ears, I pushed that fear down. My brows furrowed, and my lips pressed in a tight line as I shoved a bit more magic into my broom, giving it all I had.

Aris screamed in my ear as if I didn't know that I was racing toward my doom. Beth Ann was either smarter than me or less determined as she slowed her descent before I did. As I rocketed past her, I only had a second to bask in the fact that I was winning before I had to pull up or break my face on the ground.

Wind pushed against my face as I pulled up on my broom. It felt as if I were making taffy in the way the broom held back as I tried to bring it up to be parallel to the ground. My heart jumped into my throat as I barely made it. Then I was passing the finish line and the crowd was going wild. I could barely hear them over the thudding of my own heart, and I swore that I'd gained a few gray hairs after this whole thing. But I'd won. I'd beaten Beth Ann. Even with her cheating. I'd won!

Chapter 18

VALENTINE'S DAY WAS ALMOST upon us, and that meant the second game was to be shortly after. I could say that I was more nervous about this one than the last. Especially since it would be a partnered event to go along with the holiday, and my partner was none other than Ian Broomstein.

"Are you going to tell me where you were?" I asked Ian for what felt like the millionth time since the first game. I shifted in my seat at the restaurant we'd gone to for Valentine's day. Since I had four men in my life, we had to handle things like this in a different manner. Sometimes we did a group outing, and other times, depending on if it was wanted, we did separate dates, one for each man. This time around, I had been the one to request to see them each separately, not only to resolidify my love for each of them, but because I wanted to talk to Ian alone.

Since the first game, we hadn't had much time alone. Either one or both of us were busy with school or something else would get in the way. And when I said something, I meant someone—Beth Ann. Everywhere I turned, there she was, making a nuisance of herself. We'd even tried to hide away in his bedroom, but not long afterward someone would come calling on Ian in desperate need of his help with something.

It was really starting to piss me off.

But today she couldn't have him. Today was my day. I had plans for each of the guys this week, one date a night based on each of our schedules. Tonight was Ian's night.

Ian glanced up from his steak, his lips tugging up at the edges. "I told you. I got caught up in work, that's all."

I hummed and lifted my wine glass to my lips. I didn't want to think that Ian was lying to me, but I knew he wasn't telling me the whole truth. It made my stomach ache to think of what he might be keeping from me, but no matter how I tried to word the question, I'd always get the same vague answer.

"I'm just sorry you missed my glorious victory. You should have seen Beth Ann's face when I beat her." I offered him a smile and tried to put our date back on track.

Though I had won my race against Beth Ann, the thrill of it had been short-lived on the back of Ian still not making an appearance for Aidan's, Dale's, and Paul's races. The guys dominated the field, each of them winning their races without a problem.

Of course, they weren't up against their nemesis, so I'd say that put things to their advantage, not that they needed it. I couldn't stop watching them as they moved through the obstacles as if they were nothing. Each of them was like a knight on a gallant steed with how at ease they were on their brooms. If only Ian had been there.

"I heard." Ian grinned and picked up his phone, shaking it slightly. "I even saw it. Your mother made sure to record it and has been showing any and everyone how great of a racer her baby girl is after only a semester of lessons."

I flushed in embarrassment. "Oh, Morgana. She sure does latch on to something, doesn't she? I'm just surprised it was her and not my grandmother. She's more likely to take out a television spot just to broadcast it to the whole magical world."

Ian and laughed as we continued to eat our meal. The restaurant we had chosen this time was a human one. The decor was all decked out for Valentine's Day over the usual Italian atmosphere. The smell of freshly baked bread filled the room, and the lights were dim above with flickering little candles on each table inside of a fishbowl center centerpiece.

"What are you thinking about?" Ian cocked his head to the side, his dark hair falling in his eyes. I wanted to reach out and brush it back with my hand, so I did. Ian caught it and kissed my palm before releasing me.

I sat back in my seat and sighed. "I love the magical world, but I was just thinking that I do miss human things."

"Really? Like what?" Ian asked as he cut into his steak once more. I watched his fingers as they moved, a mesmerizing combination that made me want them on my body instead.

"The simple act of using a fork and knife to cut your meat over using a spell, for instance," I began. Ian paused mid-cut to look at me curiously. I gestured to a waiter passing by. "The way an actual person takes your order rather than the dishes taking control." When Ian frowned, I quickly added, "Not that there was anything wrong with it, but it does make me nostalgic for my old life. There were things that the magical world does better, but there are also things that you all take for granted."

"I see." Ian placed his utensils down and laced his hands in front of him. "Do enlighten me."

I gave a small, coy smile as my fingers found the neckline of the dress I'd worn for tonight. It was a deep burgundy number made of satin and lace. The straps were a few inches thick, but the neckline dipped so that my cleavage was displayed in such a way to pull the eye to it.

With a low, sultry voice, I murmured, "Like the simple act of taking your lover's clothes off. More often than not when we're with each other, we're in such a hurry to get to the main event that we never slow down long enough to even take the time to know each other's bodies. To unwrap each other, one part at a time, enjoying the unveiling as much as the act itself." I paused, my eyes locking with his heated ones. "You have to admit there is something sexy about it. The waiting."

"Yes, there is." Ian swallowed thickly, taking a drink as his eyes followed my hands while I touched my neck and shoulders. "I wouldn't be hard pressed to say no to doing some things the human way. All you had to do was ask."

I smirked and peered up at him from beneath my lashes. "Well then, I guess that means we need to practice... to make perfect, you know."

Almost knocking his cup off the table, Ian's hand jerked into the air and he croaked out, "Check!"

The rest of this week was filled with dates from my other boyfriends and each of them ended in a similar manner. Dinner or a movie, and then a night of lovemaking, each of us unable to get enough of the other's bodies. We didn't always do it in my room. In fact, I tried not to when I could because of Trina, but some of the places we did it in weren't exactly... legal.

"What is that smile on your face about?" Dale asked the morning of the second game, his own lips quirking up at the edges. He was helping me prepare my potions for the final game. We were set up in the potion's lab where the administration had their floating camera moving around the room, watching each group to be sure we weren't cheating. Dale was only allowed to hand me things, not instruct me in any manner. This was a test of how well I could brew a potion, after all.

At his question, I bit my lip and ducked my head. "Nothing. Just remembering earlier this week when we..." I trailed off, letting him fill in the blanks as I continued to put the ingredients in the potion I was brewing.

Dale handed me the next item on my list, crushed frog's brain, and then snuck up behind me, his mouth skimming my ear to avoid being overheard. "You mean when I took you into the Headmaster's office and bent you over the back of his desk? Is that the event plaguing your mind?"

I grinned despite myself and nodded. "Yes. That." I tried to focus as I measured out the precise amount needed for the potion, but it was hard with Dale's hot breath on my ear and his hands teasing my hips. We were in the potion's lab where the rest of the contestants for the second game were preparing, so it wasn't like we were alone. We couldn't just reenact the other night right here and now, no matter how much I wanted to.

"If you're worried about getting in trouble, we won't. I covered our tracks and the Headmaster doesn't use modern technology like cameras, only spells. Spells that I have access to." Dale brushed my hair away from my neck before nipping lightly at my neck. He reached over me to grab the ladle just before the cauldron started to boil. "Don't let it burn."

I turned my head toward him with a scoff. "Am I doing this, or are you? I believe it's my potion, and if you help too much, they'll think I'm cheating." I nodded my head toward the judges walking around the room to make sure no one was breaking the rules.

The second game consisted of two parts. The first part centered around potion making by the first member of the team. These potions would then be used by their partner to navigate the second part of the event, an obstacle course with far greater dangers than flying a broom through a hoop. We're talking things like walking through fire and getting across a pool of piranhas.

The real challenge was that the team members couldn't communicate. The second team member had no idea exactly what each potion would do or how it would help them navigate the course. It turned the event into a combination of potion making skills, foresight, trust, and knowledge of your partner. Since Ian and I were lovers, we should have a slight advantage in that department. Most of the other teams had only known each other a short while, and none of them were involved the way we were. My only main concern was whether or not Ian would show up this time.

"Fine, fine." Dale released me and stepped back, holding his hands up. "I won't help. I'll just sit over here and watch you."

I arched a brow at him as I poured the potion into the vial and popped the cork into it. "If you keep undressing me with your eyes, I won't be able to make this next potion right, and you could risk me killing Ian."

Dale snorted and crossed his arms over his button-down shirt. "Like you could mess up an invisibility potion."

"Shhh." I reached over and smacked him on the arm as my eyes went to those around us. While the obstacle course was the same for every team, what potions we brewed to beat it were up to each brewer. I didn't want to give the other teams an unfair advantage by overhearing my own plans.

"And I could, you know," I pointed out with narrowed eyes. "Maybe I overcook it, and it doesn't work at all. Or I add too much nitrate, and it works for only ten seconds rather than the full time he needs."

"You worry too much. That won't happen." Dale adjusted his safety glasses so he could fix his regular ones beneath the strap of the glasses, making his hair poke out in funny angles. "You wouldn't do anything that might harm Ian."

I snorted. "I wish I could say the same thing for him."

"What do you mean?"

As I chewed on my lower lip, I shook my head. "Nothing. Just a thought I had."

"Max," Dale reached out a hand, "tell me."

"He's hiding something. I don't know what, but I know he is and I'm afraid..." I let out a long sigh and rubbed a hand over my face. "I'm afraid it's something his parents pushed him into, and it's going to get him hurt or worse, killed."

Dale bobbed his head in response. "I know. I've seen how he's been lately. We all have, but Aidan's also in the Dark Arts, and he doesn't seem all that worried. So, I would think that you shouldn't be either."

"But he missed the first game. He loves races. Paul and Aidan said so." I shook my head and swallowed down my emotions. "I just don't know what to do. What if he doesn't show up today? What do we do then?"

Dale smoothed his thumb across my hand and lowered his voice. "Then Paul can take his place. I can't because I'm here as your brew assistant, and you made the potions for someone of Ian's size, not Aidan's."

I nodded in understanding. "Paul would have to do it. They won't work on anyone else."

"So, don't worry about the game," Dale reassured me with his voice and his touch, and I found myself calming a bit. "Just get through this bit, and the rest will fall into place. You'll see."

As I finished up the final potion, I tried to keep my nerves under control, but worry gnawed at my stomach, and I couldn't help but feel like Ian wasn't coming. Not to this game or the next one. That gut feeling told me more than anything else that something was wrong. I just didn't know what yet.

After I finished the potions, Dale helped me clean my station and gather them up to take out to the course on the athletic field. Each bottle was labeled for each contestant so there wouldn't be any mix-up as to the order of use.

Dale had told me one time someone had tried to cheat and use someone else's potion, but it ended up backfiring on them because the potion was made for a woman and the drinker was a man. There were many different factors to consider when making transformation potions, and one of those was the sex of the user. You'd think magic wouldn't care so much about biology, but in some ways, magic and science were really closely connected. The guy ended up in the hospital for a week and obviously didn't finish the game or any other one. No one else has tried to cheat in that manner since.

The crowd was just as wild as it was for the first event. My parents and grandparents had shown up once more and this time, since I wasn't actively taking part in the second game, I could sit with them and cheer Ian on. However, when I approached the stands and saw Aidan sitting there with them with a pinched expression on his face, I knew my predictions for the day were coming true.

"Let me guess..." I drew out my words, heavy with annoyance. "Ian is busy."

Aidan grunted, his arms crossed over his chest. He kept his pale blue eyes on the field where Paul was already down there, preparing to take part in the coming event.

I sighed and flopped down next to him. "What's going on with him Aidan? Surely, you know something."

Aidan's eyes didn't waver from the field for a few moments, but eventually, he cracked and his gaze moved to me. There was a sadness there, and a degree of guilt that I didn't like. He knew something, I could tell, but whatever it was, he wasn't going to tell me, I could see it in his face and the way he wanted to say something, but he was holding back.

"I promised," Aidan mumbled low enough that I barely heard him. "A magical binding. I can't... I can't tell you."

Scowling with frustration, I placed my feet on the metal bleachers in front of me and leaned my elbows on my knees. "God help me the day I ever learned about magic."

"Oh, honey." Mom wrapped an arm around my shoulders from behind. "You don't mean that. Magic can be a pain sometimes, but it's not all that bad. Is it?"

I gave my mom a weak smile, patting her arm until she let me go. "No, Mom. It's not all that bad."

"The game's about to start." Dad gestured toward the field, his hand full of popcorn that he popped into his mouth seconds later. "So, I get what's going to happen, but how do you tell who won? I mean, several of them could win by the end, right?"

Dale sat down next to me at that moment, sans protective glasses, and his auburn hair returned to its usual messy mop. "This event doesn't just depend on one team. The points are tallied based on how many students from each school wins their matches, then whoever has the most points by the end wins."

"What if there's a tie?" Dad asked, his calculating eyes scanning over every inch of the field. That archaeologist part of him was documenting each aspect of the culture around him like the scholar that he was. I had no doubt that, before long, he would be trying to get permission to write a book or at least a report on the magical community if he hadn't already.

Dale shrugged. "It hasn't happened yet. The last game is usually the deciding factor in it all."

"Why's that?" I inquired as I turned my gaze from Paul on the field to Dale.

With a grin and wink, Dale bumped his shoulder against mine. "You'll see. Now watch." He gestured toward the field as they lined up the contestants.

Unlike the first game, two people from each school were on a team. I had argued that Paul should have done it with Ian since he was the potions major, but Paul claimed I knew his brother's mind better than he did. Since they hadn't been exactly talking to each other until this last year, I guessed that was true.

"Were they mad that Ian wasn't here?" I asked Aidan as I looked away from the first obstacle. This was an easy one. Find a way over or through a raging wall of fire that spread across the middle of the field horizontally. No spells could be used, just the potions the partners made beforehand.

Aidan shook his head. "No, Paul dealt with it."

I hummed. I had a feeling that a lot of the animosity between the two brothers before I had come along had to do with Ian leaving Paul to clean up his messes. If it was a bad habit Ian was falling back on, I'd have to make sure it was remedied quickly. I couldn't have them fighting, or it wouldn't work for us. I wasn't sure my heart could take choosing between them.

Paul found my vial and tipped it back without a second thought. It warmed my chest that he trusted me so completely. I didn't know anyone else that would just toss back what could be a lethal dosage with such ease.

The potion I'd chosen for this obstacle was the obvious choice, but it was a difficult one to brew, a potion of inflammability. I wouldn't be surprised if many of the other competitors had tried to recreate it as well, but as I watched the others take their potions and down them, I realized no one else had successfully made one like mine. Those who had taken their potions and promptly became ill were rushed off the field, while Paul cautiously approached the fire.

"How does he know what it does?" my dad asked, leaning forward between Dale and me to be heard. "He doesn't look any different."

"It's about trust, Wesley," my grandmother, Nina, answered from where she sat on the other side of my mother with my grandfather. "And a bit of brains. He has to figure out what's different about his body, like that gentleman there." She pointed at one of the contestants who just tested out jumping before he realized the potion he'd taken had given him the ability to jump over the fire.

"Ah, I see," my dad replied, grinning from ear to ear. "So, what did you do, Max?"

"Just watch," I told him as Paul came to the conclusion that he couldn't jump over the flames. He moved toward the wall of flames where it sat in the middle of the first portion and cautiously moved his hand closer to it. When he realized his hand wasn't burning, he put it all the way in. It didn't take long after that for Paul to jog through the flaming wall and to the other side.

"Magical flame retardant," my dad mused. "Very nifty."

I chuckled. "Something like that."

We grew silent as we watched the contestants move to the next obstacle. This one was trickier than the fire. They had to swim across a long portion of the field in a pool of piranhas. So, it was a mixture of speed and survival. There had been more restrictions on this one as well. They had to touch the water in some way. They couldn't just fly over it or go around. The potion I'd chosen would help Paul with both, I hoped.

Like before, Paul chugged the potion without a thought and turned to the pool. His face pinched with pain and he doubled over. My family gasped but I waved them off, watching him as his skin changed colors and he grew scales. His face elongated and sharp, snapping teeth filled his mouth. Before he even finished changing, Paul jumped into the pool and started to make his way across.

"An alligator transformation potion!" my grandfather cried with a joyous sound. "What a good idea, Max! They'll keep those little buggers away for sure."

"Thanks," I said absently, all of my attention focused on Paul. He raced across the water, snapping those jaws of his at anything that came near him. The potion would only last for a few minutes, so he had to get across before it wore off. Too bad my guardian light couldn't leave my side to help him fight off the piranhas or at least give him a heads up. She was tied to me and me alone.

The other students had done some pretty nifty—as my grandfather had said—potions to get past this obstacle themselves. Some of them were transformation potions similar to the one I had given Paul, one a turtle and the other a large fish, the latter not doing much to dissuade the piranhas. Someone else had made their body light enough to walk across the top of the water to try to bypass the whole thing all together. A quick look told me it was one of the Bluebonnets. Of course, they wouldn't want to get their feet wet. I rolled my eyes inwardly at the way she daintily walked across the pool to the other side just as Paul climbed up on the edge.

Paul's alligator form shuddered and convulsed changing him back into his normal, glorious self, just seconds after getting out of the water.

"Talk about a close call." Dale bumped my shoulder once more, and I gave him a weak smile in return.

It had been close and while I was anxious about the outcome, my mind drifted to Ian once more. I kept thinking of Ian and where he might be. What was he doing? I wanted to go search for him, but if I left, then we would forfeit the game. Both contestants had to be present to keep from cheating or whatever.

The crowd grew more anxious as two more contestants were cut out of the event, leaving only three left for the final obstacle. I leaned forward once more, my eyes locking on Paul. This last one had been the most challenging of the three to figure out. The event organizers didn't make it an easy one, that was for sure. I had almost given up on it because the potion I made required you to brew it overnight, and I wasn't sure if they would let me prep that far in advance.

"Don't worry." Dale rubbed my back and murmured in my ear, "It'll work. It has to."

I chewed on my nails as I watched Paul down the next potion. The next obstacle required precision and patience. You couldn't just barrel through it like the others. A glass corridor stood before the contestants. It looked perfectly harmless, just a short hallway on the way to their prize. Eight of them sat side by side. One for each contestant. Well, three of them since the other five had been disqualified.

As they stepped up to the hallway, one of the contestants, the other male there who had been changed into a turtle, grabbed his head. He screamed as something happened to him, too far away for us to see.

"It's his eyes," my mom explained, holding up a pair of binoculars. "The potion was an eye opener. It helps to see those things that are unseen."

Fuck. Why didn't I think of that one?

"What one did you do, Max?" my grandmother asked, her eyes never moving from the scene before us. It was like a train wreck to be sure. A horrible, horrible train wreck that you both wanted to watch and pull your eyes away from because the anxiety of it all was just too much.

Swallowing, I licked my lips and said, "Not that one. Another one. It heightens the five senses to the point that it practically gives you a sixth sense. An ability to sense danger. A bit like..." I tried to figure out how to explain it to them.

"Spider Man," Aidan finished for me and I smiled up at him.

"Yes, like Spider Man."

Just then, a loud scream pierced the air. Every eye in the bleachers turned to the field below. The Bluebonnet was the one screaming, clutching her hand and falling back out of the glass corridor and onto the grass as blood spurted from her finger. Her missing finger. A silver blade slid back into the place and disappeared in the glass wall of the hallway she'd just tried to enter.

"Stupid girl, trying to feel your way through." A lady in front of us clucked her tongue and shook her head. "They better find her finger if they want to attach it in time." Her companions agreed with her, but I couldn't be bothered on the matter. I felt bad for her sure, but I cared more about making sure my guy didn't end up in pieces like her.

Paul slowly approached the hallway, but unlike the Bluebonnet, he didn't put his hand out in front of him to test the path. He paused only one step in, then took a deep breath before blowing it out before him. All at once, several circular blades darted across the path, leaving only a small safe zone to stand in between them. It was quite obvious what the game makers had intended for him to do. I just hoped the added benefit of my potion would help him keep from slicing an important bit off before he made it through.

I didn't pay any mind to the other contestant, entirely focused on Paul and seeing him make it. Paul, the patient guy that he was, blew out another long mouthful of air. The blades darted out again, but just before they flew back into their places, he moved. He did this again for the next section and then next, each time his puffs of air revealing another set of deadly blades to navigate, until he came to the final stretch of hallway. This time, his blowing air out didn't result in any obvious traps, but unlike his competition, he didn't try to walk right through.

The agonizing scream of the Mountaineer filled the air as a circular saw came out and cut him down at the knees. Immediately, the healers came rushing in. Someone spelled the hallway to stop as they dragged the Mountaineer away, leaving Paul as the last and only contestant.

Paul, having noticed the Mountaineer's unlegging, moved slowly so as not to cause any wind as he leaned down and blew across the lower half of the walkway. The saw that had maimed the Mountaineer came out quick as could be. There was no clear gap on this one, though, both in timing or in walk space. Paul would have to jump if he wanted to get across with his legs enact.

"Oh, Merlin," Mom gasped as she grabbed my shoulders and held on tightly as we watched. My muscles were tight, and my jaw ached from clenching it. I knew I shouldn't worry. They could put the other guy back together, so if Paul messed up, he wouldn't die, but still, who wanted to see their lover cut apart? It had to be an agonizing ordeal, and part of me wondered how it was even legal.

My dad voiced such a concern. "How is this even legal?"

"They have to sign a waiver before going through the games," my grandfather explained over my mom and grandmother. "There is rarely an event where someone doesn't come out bloody or missing a limb. Why, in my day, when I competed, I lost my sight for a whole week." He chuckled like it was no big deal. While it might not have been in the long run, right now, it seemed like a very real deal.

A hush fell over the field and bleachers as we all watched to see if Paul would make it. His fingers curled and uncurled as he seemed to be gearing himself up for it. He had to jump quite high without any room to run to build up momentum. It kind of made me wish I'd given him the jumping ability from the first obstacle.

But Paul surprised us all. Instead of trying to jump straight over it, he put his hands up on one side of the hallway and then his legs up on the other side, bracing himself so he was suspended only by his hands and feet over the pathway of doom. After he took a moment to ensure he was steady, Paul began to inch his hands and feet forward until he was above where the blade would come out. That's when his foot almost slipped.

I swore my heart stopped as I braced myself for seeing him cut to pieces... but at the last second, Paul used the momentum of his impending fall to flip his body out of the hallway and onto the grass beyond.

Cheers erupted throughout the field, and I found myself on my feet and rushing down the bleachers before I knew it. I had to see Paul and wrap my arms around him. I needed to know with my body that he was truly and irrevocably safe.

It was harder to get to him than I thought it would be. Everyone else wanted to get down there and congratulate him or check on their own contestants, and it was minutes before I got to his side. When I did though, I pushed past the examiner and threw myself into his arms.

"Oh, my God, Paul! I was so scared! I thought you were going to get hurt for sure."

Paul chuckled and held me close. "I did too, for a moment there. I won't be thanking my brother for skipping out on this ordeal anytime soon. In fact, he's going to owe me big time."

I laughed with a mixture of relief and just a wee bit of hysteria as I kissed his face and held him tight. Ian definitely owed Paul for this one, but then again, he would be the one who had to face the trials, and I wasn't a hundred percent sure that he would have been able to pull it off the same way.

As it was, the fates were in our favor today, regardless of who played the part.

Chapter 19

THE LAST GAME WAS so close I could taste it, but first, I had to deal with finals. Nothing haunted my dreams more than a multiple-choice test. I'd have rather watched Paul, Ian, and the whole lot of them go through the last game again than try to figure out a true or false answer.

Speaking of Ian... the jerk came strolling in to the second game celebration like he hadn't just up and left us hanging high and dry. The guys and I were sitting together in the quad where the Headmaster was going around congratulating the students and asking about everyone's wellbeing. I could tell the old man was preening from our latest win by the way he kept smacking Paul and me on the back, and talking about the good old days.

"And this young man," Headmaster Swordson cried out as Ian strolled up to our group, "where have you been? Your brother put on quite a show. Quite a show indeed." He laughed and clapped Paul on the shoulder once more, hard enough to make him wince.

I held back a smile at how uncomfortable Paul was with all the attention as he nodded and smiled at the Headmaster.

Ian scanned our faces, pausing on mine before he turned to the Headmaster. "An unfortunate turn of events caused me to be detained. I heard that I missed a lot of excitement."

"You missed a lot more than that," I bit out between my teeth as my hand tightened on my red Solo cup. Dale, who sat to my left on a couch they had conjured up for the occasion, placed his hand on my thigh and gave me a reassuring squeeze.

Ian's shoulders bunched up around his ears as he avoided my gaze. For a moment, I thought he'd tell me where he'd been but...

"Pencils down," my divination professor called out, jolting me out of my thoughts.

I sighed and let go of my test so it could float up to the professor's awaiting hands. At least Ian had the decency to look contrite, not that he had given me any answers about his whereabouts after that or any of the days since then. Aidan had been as quiet about it as ever, but seeing as he was magically bound to keep Ian's secret, I couldn't put too much blame on him.

So, maybe I was punishing Ian for holding back, and leaving Paul and me high and dry.

Maybe I was giving him the silent treatment for the last two months. Could you blame me? He dodged my questions without so much of a how do you do. I understood that he had to keep things secret for his schoolwork, but when it started to affect our relationship, then enough was enough.

"How'd it go?" Paul asked when I appeared in the cafeteria a short while later. He and Dale sat at a round table, their trays already loaded with food.

I shifted in my seat, laying my face on my hand with a groan.

"That good, huh?" Dale chuckled as he popped a fry into his mouth.

My nose crinkled up in disgust. "I don't know how you can eat right now. Tests always make me queasy."

Dale shrugged and took a big bite of his pizza. "I like tests. They're riveting. Makes me build up an appetite."

I eyed his overflowing tray and arched a brow. "I can tell. How about you?" I glanced over at Paul. "Do tests get you hard?"

Dale choked on his soda. He coughed and beat his chest as he gasped for air. "I never said that," he croaked between breaths as his eyes watered.

I wrinkled my nose at him. "You didn't have to. Your nerd boner is visible from here, babe."

"Why you..." Dale growled, his eyes flashing with mischief.

Paul laughed as Dale reached over and grabbed at my sides, tickling me until I begged him to stop. I ended up in his lap somehow, where something hard poked me in the butt.

"I might be a bit jealous." I wiggled with a coy smile. "I don't know if this is for me or for your teacher."

Dale groaned and held me tight to his lap. "You... Definitely you."

As we laughed and joked, Aidan and Ian walked up to our table. My laughter died as I locked eyes with Ian and then quickly turned my gaze to Dale. As I stroked my fingers through his hair, I murmured, "You need a haircut."

Dale's eyes drifted from Ian to me and back again, before he settled on me. "Want to do it for me?"

I laughed harshly. "Not unless you want to bleed."

"Yeah, trusting Max with scissors near your head... not a good idea." Ian chuckled as he and Aidan took a seat across on the other side of the table.

That easy laugh didn't disarm my anger with Ian, so I turned my gaze to Aidan instead. "How were finals? Make anyone cry during the flying test?"

Aidan's lips twitched. "No."

"Of course not." Ian clapped Aidan on the shoulder and grinned. "You should know by now this guy is a big softy. He'd let Merlin himself use him as a human shield if he asked."

"So, that means it's alright to use him that way too?" I snapped as I finally spun toward Ian. "Because he'll let you? Is that what you're saying, Ian?"

Ian's smile fell, and he stumbled over his words. "No, I didn't mean that. I just meant—"

"What?" I interrupted. "You just meant what? That since he's your friend, he wouldn't care if you forced him to keep your secrets?"

"Max," Paul mumbled next to my empty chair. "Let's not do this here."

I ignored him, glaring full out at his brother. "Did you ever think once that your secret could hurt him in other ways? That it would put a strain between us?"

"No, I..." Ian stuttered as he spoke. "Max, you have to understand..."

"No, I don't!" I snapped and stood up as I shook my head. "I'm tired of trying to understand. You keep your secrets, okay? Just let me know when you want to be part of this relationship again."

"Max..." Dale tried to reach for my hands, but I pushed him off.

"No, I'm going to go. I still have to pack and get ready for tomorrow." My eyes shot to Ian and narrowed. "Some of us are still trying to win this thing."

I didn't wait for a response. Instead, I turned on my heels and marched through the cafeteria. I only got as far as the hallway before a hand grabbed my elbow. I spun around, expecting to see Paul or Dale trying to appease me, but when I saw Ian, all I wanted to do was scream.

"Go away." I turned back around and kept walking, but Ian kept step with me. "I don't want to talk to you."

"Good," he replied. "I don't want to hear you yell at me some more. So, you can just listen." Out of the corner of my eye, I watched Ian tuck his hands into his pockets, his eyes focused straight ahead.

"What makes you think I want to hear what you have to say?" I shot back, my voice as hard as ice. "If you're just going to give me more vague non-answers, then save your breath. I don't want to hear them."

Ian shrugged. "Maybe not, but I'm going to say it anyway."

We walked for a bit more before Ian actually spoke again. When he did, even though I told him that I didn't want to hear it, my ears strained for every word.

"Look, I know this is hard," he began slowly and thoughtfully. "It's hard for me too, but the profession I want to get into requires me to be secretive about my work until I can reveal it to the public. There are so many witches and wizards out there that would kill to figure out what I'm working on, to get any kind of breakthrough that would lead them to infamy in the Dark Arts. I can't risk it getting out before I have succeeded."

I heard what he was saying, and I understood everything… but it didn't make it any better. At the end of it all, the one thing I got out of that was that he didn't trust me. Ian didn't trust me to keep my mouth shut about it. Hell, he didn't even trust Aidan since he made him undergo a magical pact to ensure his silence.

"That's sad, Ian," I finally said after a moment, shaking my head as I chewed my lower lip.

"Why?" he asked in confusion. "I'm doing what I love."

"At what cost?" I countered, stopping to look at him. "If you have to cut off everyone in your life to make something of yourself in this profession, is it really worth it?"

Ian opened his mouth to retort, but then he clamped it shut, his brows furrowing. "I don't know."

I gave a small, pitiful smile. "Well, then I guess until you do, this is it for us. I won't be pushed away like this, to be put second all the time. Especially for something you won't even share with me."

"But Max..." Ian grabbed for me, but I backed away, unable to bear him holding me to do what I needed to do. "I love you."

Tears burned my eyes as I shook my head and wrapped my arms around myself. "Not enough to trust me. I'm sorry." I twisted away from him and ran down the hallway, no longer caring if people stared.

Thankfully, Ian didn't follow me this time. When I arrived at my room, Callie was there, waiting on my bed. Despite my confusion at her presence, there was some small relief to knowing my best friend was here right after what just happened. I wiped my eyes with the back of my hand as Callie stood up and came to me.

Without a word, she wrapped her arms around me, holding me tight. I sank into her chest and just gave in. Racking sobs filled my chest, and I let them all out, feeling completely at ease with my best friend. After all, she had seen me at my worst and would never judge me for anything I did, even crying over a guy.

After I cried my heart out, I sniffed and wiped my eyes. "Not that I'm not happy to see you, Cal, but what are you doing here?"

Callie leaned back from me and smiled shyly. I'd never seen her that way before. My

Callie was the confident, take no shit from no one type, and this one was almost bashful.

"I'm here to see Chad. We're gonna go out in a bit, but I wanted to check up on you. My best friend radar said you might need me right now."

I gave a sad laugh. "Well, it's on point."

Callie led me over to my bed and as we sat down, she turned to me. "So, tell me about it."

I sighed and explained everything. All of Ian's secretiveness. The crap with Beth Ann. Everything. It felt good to get it out. While some of it was out in the open, especially Beth Ann's worst antics, I'd been holding in so much of it for a while now, not sure how to handle it and not wanting to bother Callie. She had enough going on in her life without having to listen to me whine about my many boyfriends.

"So you and Ian broke up?"

I nodded. "Yeah, I think so."

"Are you going to get back together?" Callie cautiously asked, her dark eyes focusing on me.

I sighed and shook my head before collapsing onto my bed. "I don't know. Not until he can start trusting me. We can't be in a relationship where he holds a huge part of himself back from me."

"Maybe it's like the military?"

I sat up and frowned at her. "What?"

"You know, like special ops." Callie leaned down to lay on her elbow. "My cousin was stationed in places all over the world, but he couldn't even tell his parents where he was or what he was doing."

"That's not the same thing."

"How do you know it isn't?" she astutely pointed out. "You said he made even Aidan do a binding spell to keep his secrets, and aren't they best friends?"

I sighed. "Yeah."

"Then obviously it's not you he doesn't trust. It's everybody else," Callie mused. "If the field is as competitive as you said, then he's probably just making sure that he doesn't let anything slip. And you know how I am with secrets. If I don't keep it a secret from everyone, then I can't keep it from anyone."

I arched a brow. "And what, pray tell, are you keeping a secret about now, oh best friend of mine?"

Callie ducked her head and blushed. Like, actually blushed. She never did that!

"Callie," I drawled. "Is this about Chad?" I poked at her with a smile. "Do you lurve him?"

"Stop it." Callie pushed me away with a giggle. "And he's still engaged to the Wicked Witch of the South, remember?"

I rolled my eyes and groaned. "That poor guy. His parents must hate him to pair him with Beth Ann."

Callie snorted, rubbing her ribs with her hand. "Yeah, she's a ball and a half. I'm still sore where she tried to kill me with my own corset."

"I doubt she'd have killed you," I pointed out. "Knock you out? Yeah. But murder in the middle of a school event? Not likely. There were too many witnesses."

"Didn't keep her from trying," Callie retorted with a grimace, and then her face changed to a more serious expression. "There's something I wanted to talk to you about in any case."

"Oh yeah?" I shifted around to face her. "What is it?"

Callie played with the comforter on my bed, not meeting my eyes. "So... Chad invited me to go back to California with him."

"What?" I gasped, my eyes wide and my heart jumping into my throat. "Why? Why would you do that?"

Callie glanced up from the bed to meet my eyes. There was excitement there, but also a bit of hesitation that I hoped wasn't because of me. I hated to think she was too scared to tell me things.

"They recently added a human integration program there and he said he could help me get into it." Before I could ask more about it, she jumped right in. "It's really cool. I'd get to learn all about the magical world and even learn a few trades like potions. Maybe then I'll fit in more with you and your crowd."

"Callie," I touched her hand, speaking with a softness in my voice, "you are my crowd. No matter where I am or who I'm with, you are my number one."

Callie laughed, throwing her head back so that her dark tresses fell down her back. "It's fine, Max. Really. You have your hands full right now, you know, with all the balls you're juggling." When I arched a brow, she added a salacious wink. "And I do mean that literally. It'll be nice to have a change of scenery. You know I've always wanted to go to California, and now's my chance."

"Plus, Chad will be there?" I slyly slipped in, making her blush again. "So, what do your parents think about it?"

"You're not mad?"

I shook my head as I held her hands tightly. "Why would I be? If this is what you want to do, then go for it. It's not like I have much room to talk. I did ditch you at Brown for this place." I glanced around the room.

"Yeah. You're right. And about my parents? I haven't told them yet." She sighed and sagged into the bed. "I'm sure they're gonna flip out because I'm switching yet again to another college. The upside is that they won't have to pay for this one. They have a scholarship that comes with the program. I just have to keep my head down and not get hexed in the meantime.”

I snorted. “You? Keep your head down? When has that ever happened?”

Callie laughed. “You’re right. Never.”

“When do you leave?” I asked, after we stopped laughing. “I’m assuming you’ll be around until after the games at least.”

As she nodded, Callie pulled out her phone to look at something. “Chad wants me to come for the summer. Hang out and get to know the area before school, so I think I might go then. That way, maybe by the time school starts, I have all my homesickness out of the way.”

My eyes got misty. “Well, I’m going to miss you.”

“Oh, Max! Me too! But we’ll see each other every break and the time will fly by. You won’t even notice I’m gone.”

That I knew was a lie. I’d notice every second of it.

Chapter 20

THE DAY OF THE big event came, and I was more than ready. Out of all the events, this one would be the most physical. The rest had challenged my brain, but this one... for this one, I got to shoot people.

I scanned over my reflection one more time in my mirror, taking in the outfit I'd bought with Aidan and Ian. My chest tightened at the thought of Ian, but I pushed it away. It was for the best... I hoped.

Looking up at Aris as she hovered above me, I quirked a brow. "What do you think? Think I'll strike fear into the hearts of my enemies?"

My guardian light bobbed, and whether or not that had anything to do with my question, I took it as a yes.

"Good." I picked up my gun and held it over my shoulder with a triumphant grin. "I'm ready."

The Potion Ball event was being held in the empty woods near the campus that would be spelled off from those who didn't already know it was there. This kept the humans from accidentally wandering into the magical battlefield and ending up turned into a duck or something worse.

This event was much bigger than the others and there wasn't a live audience to cheer us on. The game would be streamed back to the school via magical divination sensors and flying cameras where everyone would watch it on a bank of monitors set up in the auditorium. That would keep all the spectators safe while also making it less likely someone would cheat by giving away the positions of the teams.

I was giddy with excitement and had to shake my hands to keep them from freaking out as I made my way to Aidan's Jeep. We were going to ride over to the field together where we'd convene before the big battle. Ian was supposed to ride with us, but when I got there, I was relieved to find that he wasn't there.

"Let me guess, he's indisposed?" I mockingly used air quotes and didn't even pretend to hide my snarl.

Aidan jerked his head in response, while Paul and Dale sat in the back seat with wary looks on their faces. I didn't know if Ian told them that I'd broken up with him the other night, and I wasn't in the mood to start crying again, so I kept my mouth shut for now. I planned to do a lot of therapeutic release today in the woods.

Then I'd deal with Ian.

Aidan drove us out of the parking lot of the school and turned onto the road. The trip was short, which was good because the tension in the car could be sliced with a knife. I didn't know if the guys were trying to be cautious around me or what, but I appreciated the quiet. I needed to keep my head in the game and not wind up in an argument with another one of them.

When we arrived at the lot near the woods, it was already packed with vehicles. People were pouring out of them to gather near the entrance gate in the wards. Aidan pulled us into a spot but before he could finish parking, I jumped out of my side of the Jeep.

I jogged over to the group of students all waiting for the Headmaster to give the beginning speech. Headmaster Swordson had dressed for the part today. Instead of his usual three piece suit, he wore a pair of grey cargo pants and a long-sleeved ribbed shirt. It looked kind of silly on the old man with the bit of a paunch around his belly and those small reading glasses. He had even marked his face with black paint on each cheek and looked far too excited for the day's events.

"Welcome! Welcome! This is the final event of this year's MagiX Games! I hope you have all had a wonderful time at our glorious Winchester Academy. It has been our pleasure to host the games this year and hope to do it again in the years to come." He let out a little chuckle. "As well as bring home a trophy or two."

The crowd laughed with him politely. Off to the sides, I could see a floating camera moving with the Headmaster, making sure to get in every single word. There were probably more in the woods, no doubt, laying in wait for us to come through. They wouldn't want to miss a single part of the game, plus they kept the contestants from cheating or using lethal potions.

The Headmaster continued on to explain the rules of this event. "As you know, there will be one team for each school. You will tie your school's marker on your left arm. It is up to you to be sure to know who you are firing upon before shooting." His eyes grew serious as he scanned the lot of us. "In the real world, you can never be sure who is your friend and who is your foe. There will be no exceptions. If you are out by one of your own, then you are out. Now..." He paused for emphasis. "The goal is to be the last one standing. Whichever team is left when all the others have fallen wins. If there is a tie by the end of the day when the whistle is blown, whoever has the most players left will be declared the winner."

The crowd of students began to get restless. Each of us was more than ready to get into position and start taking our opponents out. Without realizing I was doing it, I searched Beth Ann and her Bluebonnets out in the crowd. She stood in a hot pink and black outfit, much like the one that Ian had wanted me to wear. Her red hair was pulled back into a long ponytail, and her manicured nails held onto her gun so daintily that I wondered if she even knew how to use it. My own fingers curled tightly around my weapon, the urge to shoot her now almost too hard to resist.

"Hey, eyes up front, tiger." Paul placed his hand on my shoulder and his mouth at my ear. "Don't look too eager to get her."

I flicked my eyes over my shoulder and snorted. "Wasn't trying to hide it."

"Still," Paul chuckled, "it's best not to paint a target on your back from the get go."

I gritted my teeth together and bit out, "Fine."

Headmaster Swordson completed his little speech, and the crowd roared with excitement. The energy and magic in such a small area made the air crackle around us. It made it hard not to be amped up, let alone trigger-happy.

The guys and I followed the directions for our side of the woods where we and the rest of our team, which included Trina and Sabrina plus a few I didn't know, was to enter. Once we reached our designated entrance, one of the game judges spelled each of us so that we could enter and leave the game area freely. Since Winchester Academy was winning, we were allowed to go into the woods before the others, to hide and strategize, then the Bluebonnets, then the Calis. Finally, whoever else was still in the game would be let in. I didn't care about them. Only the Bluebonnets. We were only beating them by a few points, so whoever won this last game would be put over the top. It would make or break us.

"Make sure you don't go out of bounds," Dale told me as we moved through the woods. We had ten minutes to get in position before the next group would come in. "If you are not in the marked grounds when the game ends, you won't count as having played. The ones you shot won't count, and you will be one less body for us."

I nodded in understanding. "Don't worry. The jaws of life couldn't get me to cross that line."

"So, why don't you girls guard the flag?" one of the guys, I think his name was Jared, suggested as he pulled his mask over his face.

"Fuck that!" Trina snapped before I could even get the words out myself. "That's so sexist. We are not going to just wait in the background while you guys get all the glory."

"Here, here!" one of the other women in our group cheered, pounding the air.

Jared tried to argue, but Paul put his hand up. "We don't have time for this. Aidan and Dale are the best at strategizing, so where do you want us?"

The two of them looked at one another and then across the area. Dale pointed at our flagpole. "Getting a flag is as important as keeping others from ours, so we need our best shooters here guarding it. That would be Aidan, Paul, and Jared. Trina and Max, you're both small and can blend in better with the terrain than Sabrina and Christy." The other girls gasped in horror, and Dale gave an apologetic shrug. "It's true... plus, who wears bright colors to a Potion Ball match?"

Sabrina glanced down at her yellow and black outfit, then shrugged as she looked at her nails. "I'm meant to stand out, not hide in the shadows."

"Which is why you will be the distractions," Dale continued. "You'll draw the others' attention away from Max and Trina so that they can get one up on the other teams. Remember, we only need one flag." Dale scanned the group and then shoved his own mask down over his face. "Move out!"

I pulled my mask over my face and touched hands with the guys before heading deeper into the woods. Trina and I moved together, keeping an eye out for any of the other contestants. Our armbands were green, and the rest of them shouldn't be anywhere near us.

"I think we should split up. There are plenty of flags to choose from. Everyone will be aiming for ours since we're winning," Trina told me as we paused by a cluster of trees. "If Sabrina and that Christy girl do their jobs, they'll drive attention toward them, leaving everyone else's flags free for the taking."

I nodded in agreement and scanned the area. There were dense trees to the back, but the front section of the forest had a lot more skinny trees. That made it both harder to hide and easier to see someone coming.

"I'll go this way." I gestured with the barrel of my gun." Circle around the back and sneak up on one of them," I explained, my palms sweating at the prospect of getting into a shooting match. It was a heady sensation. The adrenaline pumping in your veins, not knowing if you'll win or lose.

One could get addicted to it if they weren't careful.

Trina jerked her gun toward the front. "I'll go the other way. Maybe we'll head them off in the middle."

"Good luck." I smiled through my mask though she couldn't see it. We bumped fists and each headed in our respective directions.

I only moved a few feet before a whistle blew through the woods. I glanced up, I knew what the sound was. All the players were in the field. The game was about to begin.

I moved quickly through the woods, snapping twigs and jumping logs on my way. Since I was far enough into the forest, I figured I didn't have to be quiet just yet.

Minutes passed tensely. I'd been walking for a bit now, and besides the sound of shots farther behind me, the air had been pretty silent. There weren't any animals to be seen, probably scared away during the setup of the arena. I'd feel bad if I accidentally shot a rabbit with one of my shocking potion balls or worse, the paralysis one! They could get eaten because I shot them instead of Beth Ann's smug face.

My teeth gritted together at the thought of the redhead. She'd done her best to make this year as uncomfortable as possible. I couldn't imagine what would happen if she knew Ian and me weren't together anymore. She'd probably drop Chad like last week's trash. Good for Callie but bad for me.

Wait. No. I broke up with him. He was keeping secrets.

Didn't mean I didn't still love him though.

Unfortunately, that was true. I wanted to be with Ian, but I just couldn't do it if he wasn't going to be all in. While I had four of them to myself, I just couldn't see myself being second to his work or anyone else.

I was just about to change directions when I felt something. The air already had a kind of static feeling to it from the magical barrier around us, but this was different. Harsher but familiar. My brows furrowed and I found my feet moving toward the feeling instead of the flag.

The gun shots were getting closer now, but I ignored them in search of the magic nearby. It wasn't the barrier, that much I was certain of now. The barrier buzzed, and this magic was warmer, more sensual, with a hint of darkness. What was that?

I didn't realize how far I'd gone until my feet touched the line of the arena's barrier. If I crossed it, my team wouldn't get to count me if there was a tie. If I didn't, then I wouldn't know what or who was doing that magic. How much was my curiosity worth?

But what if I just go look for a second?

Dale said that I just had to be back before the game ended. The game was far from over. There was still time. I could get to whoever was doing this and back before they ever even missed me. Plus, I had no doubt in my mind that Trina would capture the flag. She had a fierceness about her that wouldn't be easily subdued.

Another pulse of magic solidified it for me. I knew why it felt so familiar. Ian. His magic had that dark sort of tinge to it with a smoky aftertaste that left me always wanting more.

My choice made, I took the final step across the line and out of bounds. Here, outside the barrier, I could feel the magic against my skin as if it were a caress of a hand. I knew within an instant whose magic it was now.

Ian.

As I raced through the woods toward the magic, questions filled my head. What was he doing out here? I thought he had work to do. Suddenly, my throat clogged with worry and distress. What if he was doing something with the Dark Arts that was dangerous to have others around. I mean, the woods weren't really the ideal spot for hardcore magic, but it was quiet and not many came out here. Except now.

Pushing those thoughts down, I figured the only way I was going to get an answer was to find out for myself. That meant I had to keep going.

With a renewed determination, my feet moved quicker than before. I searched for Ian's familiar head of hair but couldn't see him anywhere. It wasn't until I followed that trail of magic to a clearing in the trees that I saw him.

Kneeling on the ground in front of a body, Ian had his hands out in front of him, and hovering over the legs of the figure. Several others stood around him, and I recognized a few of them from the Dark Arts induction ceremony. The girl who had been so nice before, Faith, if I remembered her name right, was standing off to one side as they all watched.

None of them seemed to be helping Ian. They all simply watched. The magic buzzed in the air, getting thicker the closer I got. My eyes dropped to Ian where he sat. I then noticed the white plastic sheet on the ground and the blood spilled on it. Fresh blood.

My hand shoved my mask off my face as my skin grew damp and my stomach rolled. What was Ian doing here?

"Ian?" I called out, moving slowly toward them.

That's when Faith noticed me. She stood up and tried to intercept me. "Max, you need to get back! You can't be here."

"What is he doing?" I gasped as I tried to push past her to see. "Is that guy dead?"

"You need to leave," she reiterated without answering the question.

"No." I shook my head. "Not until Ian tells me what's going on here." I called past Faith toward Ian, yelling, "Is this what you've been doing here this whole time?"

He didn't respond. It was as if he didn't hear me.

Faith tried to push me back once more, but I shoved back... with magic. With the air already full of magic, it amplified my little mystical shove into a full-on bull rush. Faith flew through the air, and one of the other members was quick to go after her, catching her with their magic midair before she smacked into the ground. While they were otherwise occupied, I rushed to Ian's side.

I fell to the ground beside him and reached out to touch him, but his eyes were clouded over. If he was in there, he couldn't see me, and judging by my cry before, he probably couldn't even hear me. Afraid of hurting him, I dropped my gaze to the person on the ground.

The man was the contestant from the second game, the one who had his legs cut off at the knee. He wasn't dead. I could see his chest rising and falling, but his eyes were closed, his skin pale.

What was Ian doing to him?

"Don't touch him," one of the other members told me, standing by my side but not moving to remove me. "If you break his concentration you could kill them both."

My heart leapt. "What is he doing?"

"Something remarkable." Faith approached, her voice in awe as she watched Ian with a strange kind of reverence. "Something no one has done before."

I tried to figure out what exactly Ian was doing on my own since they were being cryptic about the whole damn thing. My eyes fell to the legs of the guy where Ian's eyes were focused. That was when I noticed something strange. His lower legs, the part that had been cut off, were grey, while the part above the knee was the same as the rest of his body. My brows furrowed.

"He's reattaching his legs," I observed.

"Yes," the guy next to me said.

"But that's not anything remarkable. I mean it is, but not anything a normal healer couldn't do." I chewed on my lower and tried to figure out what was wrong with this situation.

Faith kneeled on the other side of the guy and pointed at the calves. "A normal healer could reattach legs that were severed within the first twenty-four hours, but no one can bring a dead limb back to life."

My mouth dropped open. "But that's... that's crazy. Wouldn't the cells and everything be too far gone? It'd be..." I scrambled for the word, something to describe what Ian was trying to do.

"Necromancy," Faith filled in for me but then added, "Or a form of it."

I shook my head, too overwhelmed by the whole thing, and then something came to me. "Why is he doing this to him? He was hurt two months ago. The healers should have taken care of him then. Why didn't they?"

Before they could answer, the guy on the ground gasped and writhed. Ian's hands shook and sweat dripped down his face. I could practically see the magic he forced into the guy. It was similar to the way I'd healed the Headmaster's daughter. I knew he was seconds away from collapsing, and it would all be for nothing.

Before I could second guess myself, I placed my hand on Ian's shoulder. The others yelled at me, trying to stop me, but I wouldn't do it. I couldn't stop now. I had to help him.

I guided my magic into Ian, giving him my strength, my burning light to help him finish what he started. The wounded man stopped groaning in pain as the healing began in earnest, and that was enough to change the other Dark Arts students' cries of worry to encouraging cheers. I could feel our magic, mine and Ian's, moving into the legs as one, but I never removed my eyes from Ian's face.

I memorized every inch of it, every aspect that I might have missed before, as if I would never see it again. For all I knew, I wouldn't. He graduated this year, and I'd dumped him. For keeping this a secret, for not trusting me to understand.

But I did now.

This could revolutionize the way we practiced medicine. People who had no hope could finally have it. If we could reattach this guy's legs after two months, who was to say we couldn't transplant them for those who had lost them? Or even someone's eyes. The sky was the limit.

The other members were murmuring something low that I couldn't make out. My focus was all on Ian and making sure neither of us passed out.

Suddenly, my heart burst with emotion, and I let out a rasping gasp. Ian grunted shortly after me before he finally lowered his hands. His eyes fluttered open as the pull of my magic ebbed. Those swirling pools of green and brown moved down the guy and then to mine.

"Max, what are you doing here?" Ian's voice was scratchy, as if he hadn't used it in a long time. I didn't know how long they'd been here, but it had to have been several hours for him to be like this.

I gave a small smile, lifting the gun that I'd laid on the ground next to me. "There's a game going on over there." Then my eyes widened as I realized what I'd just said. "There's a game going on. Shit. Shit. I have to go." I jumped to my feet, but Ian grabbed my hand.

"Wait, Max. Please." Ian tried to stand, but he shook and fell back to the ground. I went for him before he went face first into the dirt. The guy next to him grabbed him too.

"Slow down, Ian." He told him with a gruff pull. "You just performed a medical miracle. I think you need to take a second to get your strength back."

"We did?" Ian's eyes widened, and they turned back to look at the once-injured man on the ground. "We did it, Max. We did it!"

The grey of the guy's legs was now the same color as the rest of him, flush with blood and oxygen. If I didn't know they had been severed and reattached, I wouldn't have been able to tell.

"No, you did it." I kissed him on the cheek with a grin. "I just gave you an extra boost. You did all the heavy lifting."

"Still... if you hadn't been here... I wouldn't have had the strength to do it." Ian shook his head in awe of what we had done. I was still a bit surprised too. "You have no idea how this will change the world. How much this means to me... to us." He held my hand in his, bringing it to his mouth. "I'm sorry I wasn't up front with you about what I was doing... I just didn't want anything to go wrong... and if I failed... I didn't want you to think I was a failure..."

I shook my head. "No, Ian. I understand. This is big. I get that now, and I'd never think you were anything like that." I laughed a little. "I just have to realize that I don't get to know everything in your life. Some things just have to stay yours."

"But, just so you know," he stroked my face with his hand, our mouths close together, "you were never second, Max. You could never be second. This was just a time sensitive project."

I ducked my head. "I get that now."

A whistle blew from somewhere behind me, reminding me that I was in the middle of something important too. The warning signal. They're about to do the final count.

"I really have to go, but we'll talk later. Right?"

Ian inclined his head. "I wouldn't miss it."

Kissing Ian on the mouth one more time with everything I had, I abruptly released him to run back toward the woods. I didn't know how long I had sat there with Ian, pushing power into him, but it must have been a long time if the warning call had sounded. I just hoped I got back before I was too late.

I came upon the buzzing of the barrier seconds later, and without hesitation this time, I stepped through it. Without a care for stealth now, I raced through the woods. There were students everywhere. Some of them passed out on the ground. Some were frozen in place, their guns still lifted to shoot the others. There were even a few squirrels and rabbits with school armbands, transmuted students that I knew would transform back before the game ended.

That's when Aris suddenly flared brightly and shot behind me, a clear alert that someone was coming up on my six. Her warning was just in time as I quickly dropped just as a potion ball flew over my head. It splattered against a tree in front of me, hissing as it melted the surface of the tree. I jumped to my feet, my guardian light freaking out as I dodged a few more acidic shots until I was semi-safe behind a tree.

"I'm pretty sure those are not regulation!" I called out to whoever my assailant was.

"I would imagine not." A sharp peal of laughter filled the forest, and I cringed. Fucking Beth Ann. "Of course, Swordson is too much of a softy to use any real ammunition. In Texas, we aren't afraid to bring out the big guns."

I rolled my eyes. "Does the rest of Texas know that you're a psycho?" I shouted, and then ducked around the corner to fire off three balls in the direction of her voice. I missed my initial flurry, but I was close enough that Beth Ann had to fall to the ground to avoid them. Not out of the fight yet, she returned fire with another two shots. One almost got me as I ducked back behind the tree, and my hair hissed where a little acid had splashed on the ends.

"The game's almost over, Beth Ann. Just give up," I yelled, trying to reason with her, but I knew it was all for nothing. Sabrina might have been a raging bitch, but Beth Ann made Sabrina look like Mother Teresa.

"They haven't blown the whistle yet, and even then, I have a score to settle with you," she practically hissed. "Maybe if I mark up that pretty face of yours, then you won't be so appealing to all the gentlemen you seemed to have lured into your bed."

"Lured?" I laughed, leaning my head back against the tree. "Really? I'm not a spider."

"Aren't you though?" Beth Ann questioned as her voice came closer. "My mama might have taught me to be a lady, but my daddy taught me never to leave a pest to their own business. They'll multiply, and the next thing you know... you're living in a house of iniquity."

She was trying to distract me with her words. It wouldn't work. I had her. I just needed one good shot.

"I have a rat in my presence, Maxine," Beth Ann called out with a nasty laugh, "and I intend to clean house."

Under her rant, I caught the snapping of a branch to the left, and a second later, I dropped to my knees, my gun pointed up as she jerked around the tree. The world seemed to go into slow motion. She shot off another ball... but her eyes widened as she realized I wasn't there. By the time she realized I was below her, I'd already hit her in the chest.

The potion ball splattered against her pink chest plate, the bright lime green of the potion coloring the surface. A transformation potion. Nice.

I watched with growing delight as Beth Ann shrank down. Her skin scaled over, and her face melted until she was smooth and slithering on the ground. A common garden snake. It was fitting for someone like her. All bite, but no venom. While it might hurt a little, in the end, she was just a nuisance.

I was about to turn to head back toward the front when my guardian light dinged slightly as snake Beth Ann hissed and tried to bite me. I kicked her with my black boot, only a little sorry when she vaulted through the air.

The final whistle shrieked out as I hustled to the front of the woods. I could tell right away as I entered the gathering point that my team had done well while I was helping Ian.

Trina had the Mountaineers' flag clasped in her hand, and our team had her hoisted up on their shoulders as they chanted her name. Only a couple of students from each team appeared in the clearing except for ours, while everyone but Jared and Christy had made it safe to the end.

"Well, it looks like there will not be any need for a tiebreaker," Headmaster Swordson said without even trying to hold back his glee. "Winchester Academy has won this challenge and, if my calculations are correct, the MagiX Games as well!"

Our team let out a loud cheer, and I ran into the arms of my guys. They kissed and hugged me, none of them the least bit curious as to where I had been. Still, my eyes trailed back to the woods where I had left Ian with his dream.

We'd won... in more ways than one.

Chapter 21

THE CELEBRATORY PARTY LASTED two whole days. I was pretty sure most of the students were just partying to party, because school was over and summer was here, but still, it was pretty awesome to be part of the team who won the MagiX Games.

"Are you ever going to stop staring at that?" I giggled at Trina, who sat on her bed and gazed at her trophy lovingly like it was her newfound god or something.

As she let out a long and happy sigh, Trina stroked the side of the golden statue in the shape of a broom and witch hat. "I just miss the games. The excitement. The danger. The praise."

I shook my head and laughed, folding my last article of clothing before putting it in my bag. "You're addicted to the fame, huh?"

Trina glanced away from the trophy and pinched her fingers together. "Just a bit. But can you blame me? Four siblings and not once have I ever won any of the contests we did. Either my older sisters dominated, or they let the babies win. It's nice to be appreciated."

I chuckled. "I bet. Well, next year you can compete again. I'm sure you'll be as badass as this year."

Trina grinned at me and then turned back to her trophy, her eyes glazing over. "Yeah, but there's no guarantee. This... this is definite. Already done. You should have seen me, Max. I was like Lara Croft in *Tomb Raider*. A Mad Max of Potion Ball. No one could touch me."

My cheeks ached from smiling so much. "So you've told me. Over and over and over again."

"Well, I want to be sure you know how much you missed. I mean, who gets lost in the woods? We were in a spelled bubble!" Trina threw her hands up in the air.

"I didn't get lost..." I grumbled under my breath, but I didn't explain further.

As far as everyone else knew, I'd gotten turned around and only found my way back when the game was almost over. They didn't know I'd gone out of the arena and helped Ian perform a medical miracle, a miracle that Ian had now practiced enough to replicate on his own. It was all about having enough magical power to get through the whole process. Ian could revive small pieces of the body, like a finger or an ear on his own, but anything bigger like an arm and he needed more juice than he could provide on his own. Still, he'd developed a technique that no one else had and was now being courted by some of the leading research and development teams around the world—the magical world that is.

It was quite an accomplishment and I couldn't be more proud of him.

"So, are you and Ian okay now?" Trina asked, finally moving away from the trophy to her half-packed bag. "I mean, you guys seemed like you were okay at the party where you were practically dry humping in front of everyone."

"I was not!" I threw a bundle of socks at her as my cheeks burned. "But yes, we're fine. Better than fine."

"And what about graduation?" Trina tossed my socks back at me. "How's that going to work?"

I shrugged. "The same way anyone who dates an older person does. He'll do his thing, and I'll do mine. We'll see each other on weekends, and after school and work. Same with Aidan. Both of them graduate today, you know."

"Gotcha." Trina nodded. "Well, I hope the best for you all."

"What about you and Libby? Any plans for the summer?" I sat down on my bed with a flop. We had a little bit of time before the graduation ceremony, so I was trying to get all my stuff ready before then. Who knew what we would be doing afterward?

At the mention of Libby, Trina smiled. "We're going to her parents for the summer. They have a beach house in Malibu. Sun, the beach, itty-bitty bikinis. It's going to be a blast." Trina wagged her brows suggestively, and we both fell into a fit of laughter.

A knock on my dorm room door broke up our fun. Getting out of bed, I moved over to the door and opened it.

"Dale! Hey, I thought we were going to meet downstairs." I frowned, my brows furrowed as I kissed him hello.

Dale gave me a shy smile and ran a hand through his shaggy auburn hair. "Yeah, I know, but I wanted to talk to you for a second."

I glanced back at Trina and then to Dale. "Uh, sure. Let's step out here. Trina wants a minute alone with her trophy." I wiggled my eyebrows at her, making her scowl and grab her trophy. She threw it in her bag as I closed the door behind me. I leaned against it and focused on Dale.

"What's up?"

Dale shifted in place, his hand tucked into his pocket as he pushed up his glasses. It was so adorable how nervous he was right now. I wondered what he wanted to talk about.

"So, I was wondering... I was wondering..."

"Dale," I placed my hand on his arm, my eyes softening. "You can ask me anything, I promise. It's okay."

"I know, it's just hard. I've never felt this way about anyone before, and it's kind of a big deal for me." Dale blushed up to his ears, and I wanted to kiss him so hard right then.

"Well, I'm sure whatever it is, my answer is yes."

"What are you doing this summer break?" Dale finally got the words out, and his face was so full of hopefulness, but I was still a bit confused.

"Uh..." I cocked my head to the side as I stared at him. "Nothing that I know of. Going to my parents, I guess. Why?"

"Would you... I mean, would you consider... coming home with me? To meet my family?" Dale turned his eyes away from me as if he were too afraid to see my reaction.

My chest fluttered with nerves and surprise. He wanted me to come home with him? And meet his family? As in his parents? Wow, I'd never done that before. I mean, I'd met Aidan, Ian, and Paul's parents but it wasn't like I came home with them for the whole summer break. It was in passing, at special events or, most recently, at lunch.

Plus, going home to meet the family? That was kind of a big deal.

"Are you sure?" were the first words out of my mouth. Not yes, not I don't know, but are you sure? Way to be confident, Max.

"What do you mean, am I sure?" His shock that I even asked brushed away some of my worry. "Of course, I'm sure. I love you, Max. I want my family to meet you."

I blinked up at him and a small smile curled up my lips. "You love me?"

Dale wrapped his arms around my waist and pulled me close. "Of course, I do. Don't you...?"

"Yes!" I cried out and then blushed as I lowered my voice. "I mean, yes. I love you too. I just didn't expect you to say it so...suddenly."

"Is it really sudden though?" Dale lowered his face down to mine, nipping at my lips. "I thought I was quite blatant with how in love with you I am."

I giggled and kissed him soundly on the mouth. "Well, it's still nice to hear it aloud. I'd love to come with you to see your family."

"Great. We can leave this weekend after graduation. Do you want to go by broom or old-fashioned airplanes?" Dale rubbed his nose against mine.

My brows bunched together in confusion. "I thought you're from here? Where are we going?"

"Oh, no. My grandparents live here, not my parents. My family is back in Florida... or, more specifically, off the coast of Florida. We live in the magical community of Key Witch. It's a secret island only witches and wizards know about. It even has a whole barrier over it so humans can't find us."

"Really?" My mouth fell open, and I became even more eager to meet his family. "That sounds so cool!" Then something came to mind and my face fell. "I'll have to ask my parents about it first... but you know, I'm an adult! I can go home with my boyfriend if I want to."

Dale chuckled. "Still, I'd like to stay in your parents' good graces. Running it by them wouldn't be the worst idea."

"Well, what are we waiting for?" I grinned and grabbed his hand, dragging him down the hallway. "Let's go!"

With another school year behind me and a new adventure in front of me, I couldn't let any of the bad shit that happened get me down. After all, I was a witch, there was nothing I couldn't handle.

Epilogue

Beth Ann

THAT NO GOOD, CHEATING witch! How dare she make a fool out of me?

"Maxine Mancaster," I growled to myself as I tossed things around my room. "Who does she think she is? She's nothin' but a half-breed. What does he see in her?" I groaned and dragged my hands through my long red hair.

I was gorgeous. I knew it. Everybody knew it. And on top of that, I had something most women my age didn't have—class. I was from a good Southern family with old family money. More importantly, a magical family. We had roots all the way back to the Dark Ages for cryin' out loud!

"So, what does he see in her?" I asked my reflection, my hands on my hips and my brow scrunched together like some kind of cave man. I sighed and dropped my arms, smoothing them over my tea dress. It wasn't just Max—ugh, what an unfeminine name— that I had to worry about though. There was her human 'friend.'

Callie.

She was a piece of trouble I didn't need. My parents were dead set on me marrying Chadwick since I couldn't have Ian. We needed to get a foothold in one of the other major magical cities, and it was either in Georgia or California. Right now, as it stood, we weren't getting what we wanted from Ian, and Maxine was too much of a problem to be taken care of easily.

Now, Callie, though... A little birdie told me she was joining the human integration program at Sun Valley Academy with Chadwick. If she was separated from Maxine and her little army of men, then it would be much easier to get rid of her.

I didn't suspect that Chadwick would be a problem. He wasn't the brightest bulb in the bunch, and he did whatever his mommy and daddy told him to. It would be easy to make sure that what was going on between them was a fling and nothing more, a passing fancy. At least, it better be.

My daddy might be many things, but forgiving wasn't one of them.

As if on cue, my bedroom door opened, and my father, Sergeant Zagan Scarlette, came marching in. "Beth Ann."

"Yes, Daddy?" I hustled to stand before him, ready to hear his will.

Daddy stroked his goatee, which was the same fiery red color as my hair, and narrowed his amber eyes on me. "What is this I hear about Chadwick bringing a human girl home with him this summer?"

Crap. How did he find out so quickly?

"It's nothing, Daddy. Trust me." I gave him my best innocent look, clasping my hands in front of me. "She's just a passing fancy. She won't last the summer."

"She better not. I have plans for that boy." He scanned over me for a moment in thought. "It's really too bad you couldn't get the Broomstein boy to change his mind. We would have had a better excuse for integrating our group there than in California."

I was prepared for this. "But Daddy, there are loads of Dark Arts students in California. It won't be hard at all to convince them into your way of thinking, I don't think, sir," I finished with a stern look and a salute.

Daddy always liked it when I addressed him like one of his soldiers. We might not like humans, but that didn't mean that we didn't work alongside them if we had to. When it came to war, something my daddy thrived in, we fought with the best of them.

Daddy nodded. "And what of this half-breed you were telling me about? The Mancaster girl? I heard she's been popularizing integration." He said it like it gave him a bad taste in his mouth, moving his tongue around with a grimace. "It's already catching at a few of the academies. We can't have that. The next thing we know, they'll want us all to breed with them." He scoffed a laugh as he shook his head.

"Yes, Maxine Mancaster. She's gathered herself quite the little harem of guys, it seems." I arched a brow with a tiny smile. "And wouldn't you know? They are all from influential families." I paused and thought back to the redheaded boy. "Well, maybe not all of them, but even the Varnes are in charge of that hidden island by Florida. I heard Maxine talking about going there for the summer with him."

Daddy hummed and put his hands behind his back. "Key Witch, is it?"

"Yes, I believe so."

A slow smile crawled up my daddy's face, one that even made my skin quiver with fear. "My darling, daughter. I do believe it's time to start a little chaos."

TO BE CONTINUED...

About the Author

Erin Bedford is an otaku, recovering coffee addict, and Legend of Zelda fanatic. Her brain is so full of stories that need to be told that she must get them out or explode into a million screaming chibis. Obsessed with fairy tales and bad boys, she hasn't found a story she can't twist to match her deviant mind full of innuendos, snarky humor, and dream guys.

On the outside, she's a work from home mom and bookbinger. One the inside, she's a thirteen-year-old boy screaming to get out and tell you the pervy joke they found online. As an ex-computer programmer, she dreams of one day combining her love for writing and college credits to make the ultimate video game!

Until then, when she's not writing, Erin is devouring as many books as possible on her quest to have the biggest book gut of all time. She's written over thirty books, ranging from paranormal romance, urban fantasy, and even scifi romance.

Come chat me up!
www.erinbedford.com
Facebook.com/erinrbedford
Twitter.com/erin_bedford

Don't forget to follow me on Goodreads, Pinterest, Instagram, and YouTube!

Want to be the first to know about my new releases?
Erinbedford.com/newsletter

www.ingramcontent.com/pod-product-compliance
Lightning Source LLC
Chambersburg PA
CBHW032103180726
48284CB00002B/432